Fridrik Rafusson

ABOUT THE AUTHOR

The Franco-Czech novelist and critic MILAN KUNDERA
was born in Brno and has lived in France, his second
homeland, since 1975. He is the author of the novels
*The Joke, Farewell Waltz, Life Is Elsewhere, The Book
of Laughter and Forgetting, The Unbearable Lightness of Being,* and *Immortality,* and the short-story
collection *Laughable Loves*—all originally written in
Czech. His most recent novels *Slowness, Identity,* and
Ignorance, as well as his nonfiction works *The Art
of the Novel, Testaments Betrayed, The Curtain,* and
Encounter, were originally written in French.

BOOKS BY MILAN KUNDERA

The Joke

Laughable Loves

Life Is Elsewhere

Farewell Waltz
(EARLIER TRANSLATION: *The Farewell Party*)

The Book of Laughter and Forgetting

The Unbearable Lightness of Being

Immortality

Slowness

Identity

Ignorance

Jacques and His Master (PLAY)

The Art of the Novel (ESSAY)

Testaments Betrayed (ESSAY)

The Curtain (ESSAY)

Encounter

Milan Kundera

Laughable Loves

Translated from the Czech by
Suzanne Rappaport

HARPER ● PERENNIAL

NEW YORK ● LONDON ● TORONTO ● SYDNEY ● NEW DELHI ● AUCKLAND

HARPER ● PERENNIAL

First Harper Perennial edition published 1999.

Designed by Nora Rosansky

Library of Congress Cataloging-in-Publication Data
Kundera, Milan.
    [Směšné lásky. English]
    Laughable Loves/Milan Kundera.
        p. cm.
    Contents: Nobody will laugh—The golden apple of eternal desire—The hitchhiking game—Symposium—Let the old dead make room for the young dead—Dr. Havel after twenty years—Eduard and God.
    ISBN 978-0-06-099703-8
    1. Czech Republic—Social life and customs—Fiction.   I. Title.
PG5039.21.U6S58413   1999
891.8'6354—dc21   99-15600

HB 02.20.2024

CONTENTS

This translation was first published in 1974, revised by the author in 1987, and in 1999 once again revised, more extensively, by Aaron Asher in collaboration with the author.

Laughable
Loves

Nobody Will Laugh

1

"Pour me some more slivovitz," said Klara, and I wasn't against it. It was hardly unusual for us to open a bottle, and this time there was a genuine excuse for it: that day I had received a nice fee from an art history review for a long essay.

Publishing the essay hadn't been so easy—what I'd written was polemical and controversial. That's why my essay had previously been rejected by *Visual Arts*, where the editors were old and cautious, and had then finally been published in a less important periodical, where the editors were younger and less reflective.

The mailman brought the payment to me at the university along with another letter, an unimportant letter; in the morning in the first flush of beatitude I had hardly read it. But now, at home, when it was approaching midnight and the bottle was nearly empty, I took it off the table to amuse us.

"Esteemed comrade and—if you will permit the expression—my colleague!" I read aloud to Klara. "Please excuse me, a man whom you have never met, for writing to you. I am turning to you with a request that read the enclosed article. True, I do not know you, but I respect you as a man whose judgments, reflections, and conclusions astonish me by their agreement with the results of my own research; I am completely amazed by it. . . ." There followed greater praise of my merits and then a request: Would I kindly write a review of his article—that is, a specialist's evaluation—for *Visual Arts*, which had been underestimating and rejecting his article for more than six months. People had told him that my opinion would be decisive, so now I had become the writer's only hope, a single light in otherwise total darkness.

We made fun of Mr. Zaturecky, whose aristocratic name fascinated us; but it was just fun, fun that meant no harm, for the praise he had lavished on me, along with the excellent slivovitz, softened me. It softened me so much that in those unforgettable moments I loved the whole world. And because at that moment I didn't have anything to reward the world with, I rewarded Klara. At least with promises.

Klara was a twenty-year-old girl from a good family. What am I saying, from a good family? From an excellent family! Her father had been a bank manager, and around 1950, as a representative of the upper bourgeoisie, was exiled to the village of Celakovice, some distance from Prague. As a result his daughter's party record was bad, and she had to work as a seamstress in a large Prague dressmaking establishment. I was now sitting opposite this beautiful seamstress and trying to make her like me more by telling her lightheartedly about the advantages of a job I'd promised to get her through connections. I assured her that it was absurd for such a pretty girl to lose her beauty at a sewing machine, and I decided that she should become a model.

Klara didn't object, and we spent the night in happy understanding.

2

We pass through the present with our eyes blindfolded. We are permitted merely to sense and guess at what we are actually experiencing. Only later when the cloth is untied can we glance at the past and find out what we have experienced and what meaning it has.

That evening I thought I was drinking to my successes and didn't in the least suspect that it was the prelude to my undoing.

And because I didn't suspect anything I woke up the next day in a good mood, and while Klara was still breathing contentedly by my side, I took the article, which was attached to the letter, and skimmed through it with amused indifference.

It was called "Mikolas Ales, Master of Czech Drawing," and it really wasn't worth even the half hour of inattention I devoted to it. It was a collection of platitudes jumbled together with no sense of continuity and without the least intention of advancing through them some original thought.

Quite clearly it was pure nonsense. The very same day Dr. Kalousek, the editor of *Visual Arts* (in other respects an unusually unpleasant man), confirmed my opinion over the telephone; he called me at the university: "Say, did you get that treatise from the Zaturecky guy? Then review it. Five lecturers have already cut him to pieces, but he keeps on bugging us; he's got it into his head that you're the only genuine authority. Say in two sentences that it's crap; you know how to do that, you know how to be really venomous; and then we'll all have some peace."

But something inside me protested: why should I have to be Mr. Zaturecky's executioner? Was I the one receiving an editor's salary for this? Besides, I remembered very well that they had refused my essay at *Visual Arts* out of overcautiousness; what's more, Mr. Zaturecky's name was firmly connected in my mind with Klara, slivovitz, and a beautiful evening. And finally, I won't deny it, it's human—I could have counted on one finger the people who think me "a genuine authority": why should I lose this only one?

I closed the conversation with some clever vaguery, which Kalousek considered a promise and I an excuse. I put down the receiver firmly convinced that I would never write the piece on Mr. Zaturecky's article.

Instead I took some paper out of the drawer and wrote a letter to Mr. Zaturecky, in which I avoided any kind of judgment of his work, excusing myself by saying that my opinions on nineteenth-century art were commonly considered devious and eccentric, and therefore my intercession—especially with the editors of *Visual Arts*—would harm rather than benefit his cause. At the same time I overwhelmed Mr. Zaturecky with friendly loquacity, from which it was impossible not to detect sympathy on my part.

As soon as I had put the letter in the mailbox I forgot Mr. Zaturecky. But Mr. Zaturecky did not forget me.

3

One day when I was about to end my lecture—I am an art history lecturer at the university—there was a knock at the door; it was our secretary, Marie, a kind elderly lady who occasionally prepares coffee for me and says I'm out when there are undesirable female voices on the telephone. She put her head in the doorway and said that a gentleman was looking for me.

I'm not afraid of gentlemen, and so I took leave of the students and went good-humoredly out into the corridor. A smallish man in a shabby black suit and a white shirt bowed to me. He very respectfully informed me that he was Zaturecky.

I invited the visitor into an empty room, offered him

a chair, and began pleasantly discussing everything possible with him, for instance what a bad summer it was and what exhibitions were on in Prague. Mr. Zaturecky politely agreed with all my chatter, but he soon tried to apply every remark of mine to his article, which lay invisibly between us like an irresistible magnet.

"Nothing would make me happier than to write a review of your work," I said finally, "but as I explained to you in the letter, I am not considered an expert on the Czech nineteenth century, and in addition I'm on bad terms with the editors of *Visual Arts*, who take me for a hardened modernist, so a positive review from me could only harm you."

"Oh, you're too modest," said Mr. Zaturecky. "How can you, who are such an expert, judge your own standing so blackly! In the editorial office they told me that everything depends on your review. If you support my article they'll publish it. You're my only recourse. It's the work of three years of study and three years of toil. Everything is now in your hands."

How carelessly and from what bad masonry does a man build his excuses! I didn't know how to answer Mr. Zaturecky. I involuntarily looked at his face and noticed there not only small, ancient, and innocent spectacles staring at me, but also a powerful, deep vertical wrinkle on his forehead. In a brief moment of clairvoyance a shiver shot down my spine: This wrinkle, concentrated and stubborn, betrayed not only the intellectual torment its owner had gone through over Mikolas Ales's drawings, but also unusually strong willpower. I lost my presence of mind and failed to find any clever excuse. I knew that I wouldn't write the review, but I also knew that I didn't have the strength to say so to this pathetic little man's face.

And then I began to smile and make vague promises. Mr. Zaturecky thanked me and said that he would come again soon. We parted smiling.

In a couple of days he did come. I cleverly avoided him, but the next day I was told that he was searching for me again at the university. I realized that bad times were on the way. I went quickly to Marie so as to take appropriate steps.

"Marie dear, I beg you, if that man should come looking for me again, say that I've gone to do some research in Germany and I'll be back in a month. And you should know about this: I have, as you know, all my lectures on Tuesday and Wednesday. I'll shift them secretly to Thursday and Friday. Only the students will know about this. Don't tell anyone, and leave the schedule uncorrected. I'll have to go underground."

4

In fact Mr. Zaturecky did soon come back to look me up and was miserable when the secretary informed him that I'd suddenly gone off to Germany. "But this is not possible. The lecturer has to write a review about me. How could he go away like this?" "I don't know," said Marie. "However, he'll be back in a month." "Another month . . . ," moaned Mr. Zaturecky: "And you don't know his address in Germany?" "I don't," said Marie.

And then I had a month of peace.

But the month passed more quickly than I expected, and Mr. Zaturecky stood once again in the office. "No, he still hasn't returned," said Marie, and when she met me later about something she asked me imploringly: "Your little man was here again, what in heaven's name should I tell him?" "Tell him, Marie, that I got jaundice and I'm in the hospital in Jena." "In the hospital!" cried Mr. Zaturecky, when Marie told him the story a few days later. "It's not possible! Don't you know that the lecturer has to write a review about me!" "Mr. Zaturecky," said the secretary reproachfully, "the lecturer is lying in a hospital somewhere abroad seriously ill, and you think only about your review." Mr. Zaturecky backed down and went away, but two weeks later he was once again in the office: "I sent a registered letter to the lecturer at the hospital in Jena. The letter came back to me!" "Your little man is driving me crazy," said Marie to me the next day. "You mustn't get angry with me, but what could I say? I told him that you've come back. You have to deal with him yourself now."

I didn't get angry with Marie. She had done what she could. Besides, I was far from considering myself beaten. I knew that I was not to be caught. I lived undercover all the time. I lectured secretly on Thursday and Friday, and every Tuesday and Wednesday, crouching in the doorway of a house opposite the art history faculty, I would rejoice at the sight of Mr. Zaturecky, who kept watch outside the faculty building waiting for me to come out. I longed to put on a bowler hat and a false beard. I felt like Sherlock Holmes, like Mr. Hyde, like the Invisible Man wending his way through the city; I felt like a little boy.

One day, however, Mr. Zaturecky finally got tired of keeping watch and pounced on Marie. "Where exactly does Comrade Lecturer lecture?"

"There's the schedule," said Marie, pointing to the wall, where the times of all the lectures were laid out in exemplary fashion in a large grid.

"I see that," said Mr. Zaturecky, refusing to be put off. "Only Comrade Lecturer never lectures here on either Tuesday or Wednesday. Does he call in sick?"

"No," said Marie hesitantly.

And then the little man turned again on Marie. He reproached her for the confusion in the schedule. He inquired ironically how it was that she didn't know where every teacher was at a given time. He told her that he was going to complain about her. He shouted. He said that he was also going to complain about Comrade Lecturer, who wasn't lecturing, although he was supposed to be. He asked if the dean was in.

Unfortunately the dean was in.

Mr. Zaturecky knocked on his door and went in. Ten

minutes later he returned to Marie's office and demanded my address.

"Twenty Skalnikova Street, in Litomysl," said Marie.

"Litomysl?"

"The lecturer has only a temporary address in Prague, and he doesn't want it disclosed—"

"I'm asking you to give me the address of the lecturer's Prague apartment," cried the little man in a trembling voice.

Somehow Marie lost her presence of mind. She gave him the address of my attic, my poor little refuge, my sweet den, in which I would be caught.

5

Yes, my permanent address is in Litomysl; there I have my mother and memories of my father; I flee from Prague as often as I can and write at home in my mother's small apartment. So it happened that I kept my mother's apartment as my permanent residence and in Prague didn't manage to get myself a proper bachelor apartment, as you're supposed to, but lived in lodgings, in a small, completely private attic, whose existence I concealed as much as possible in order to prevent unnecessary meetings between undesirable guests and my transient female visitors.

For precisely these reasons I didn't enjoy the best reputation in the house. Also, during my stays in Litomysl I had several times lent my cozy little room to friends, who amused themselves only too well there, not allowing anyone in the house to get a wink of sleep. All this scandalized some of the tenants, who conducted a quiet war against me. Sometimes they had the local committee express unfavorable opinions of me, and they even handed in a complaint to the housing department.

At that time it was inconvenient for Klara to get to work from such a distance as Celakovice, and so she began to stay overnight at my place. At first she stayed timidly and as an exception, then she left one dress, then several dresses, and within a short time my two suits were crammed into a corner of the wardrobe, and my little room was transformed into a woman's boudoir.

I really liked Klara; she was beautiful; it pleased me that people turned their heads when we went out together; she was at least thirteen years younger than me, which increased the students' respect for me; I had a thousand reasons for taking good care of her. But I didn't want it to be known that she was living with me. I was afraid of rumors and gossip about us in the house; I was afraid that someone would start attacking my good old landlord, who was discreet and didn't concern himself about me; I was afraid that one day he would come to me, unhappy and with a heavy heart, and ask me to send the young lady away for the sake of his good name.

Klara had strict orders not to open the door to anyone.

One day she was alone in the house. It was a sunny day and rather stuffy in the attic. She was lounging almost naked on my couch, occupying herself with an examination of the ceiling.

Suddenly there was a pounding on the door.

There was nothing alarming in this. I didn't have a bell, so anyone who came had to knock. Klara wasn't going to let herself be disturbed by the noise and didn't stop examining the ceiling. But the pounding didn't cease; on the contrary it went on with imperturbable persistence. Klara was getting nervous. She began to imagine a man standing behind the door, a man who slowly and significantly turns up the lapels of his jacket, and who will later pounce on her demanding why she hadn't opened the door, what she was concealing, and whether she was registered at this address. A feeling of guilt seized her; she lowered her eyes from the ceiling and tried to think where she had left her dress. But the pounding continued so stubbornly that in the confusion she found nothing but my raincoat hanging in the hall. She put it on and opened the door.

Instead of an evil, querying face, she saw only a little man, who bowed. "Is the lecturer at home?"

"No, he isn't." "That's a pity," said the little man, and he apologized for having disturbed her. "The thing is that the lecturer has to write a review about me. He promised me, and it's very urgent. If you would permit it, I could at least leave him a message."

Klara gave him paper and pencil, and in the evening I read that the fate of the article about Mikolas Ales was in my hands alone, and that Mr. Zaturecky was waiting most respectfully for my review and would try to look me up again at the university.

6

The next day Marie told me how Mr. Zaturecky had threatened her, and how he had gone to complain about her; her voice trembled, and she was on the verge of tears; I flew into a rage. I realized that the secretary, who until now had been laughing at my game of hide-and-seek (though I would have bet anything that she did what she did out of kindness toward me, rather than simply from a sense of fun), was now feeling hurt and conceivably saw me as the cause of her troubles. When I also included the exposure of my attic, the ten-minute pounding on the door, and Klara's fright—my anger grew to a frenzy.

As I was walking back and forth in Marie's office, biting my lips, boiling with rage, and thinking about revenge, the door opened and Mr. Zaturecky appeared.

When he saw me a glimmer of happiness flashed over his face. He bowed and greeted me.

He had come a little prematurely, before I had managed to consider my revenge.

He asked if I had received his message yesterday.

I was silent.

He repeated his question.

"I received it," I replied.

"And will you please write the review?"

I saw him in front of me: sickly, obstinate, beseeching; I saw the vertical wrinkle etched on his forehead, the line of a single passion; I examined this line and grasped that it was a straight line determined by two points: his article and my review; that beyond the vice of this maniacal straight line nothing existed in his life but saintly asceticism. And then a spiteful trick occurred to me.

"I hope you understand that after yesterday I can't speak to you," I said.

"I don't understand you."

"Don't pretend; she told me everything. You don't have to deny it."

"I don't understand you," repeated the little man, this time more decidedly.

I assumed a genial, almost friendly tone. "Look here, Mr. Zaturecky, I don't blame you. I am also a womanizer, and I understand you. In your position I would have tried to seduce a beautiful girl like that, if I'd found myself alone in an apartment with her and she'd been naked beneath a man's raincoat."

"This is an outrage!" The little man turned pale.

"No, it's the truth, Mr. Zaturecky."

"Did the lady tell you this?"

"She has no secrets from me."

16

"Comrade Lecturer, this is an outrage! I'm a married man. I have a wife! I have children!" The little man took a step forward so that I had to step back.

"So much the worse for you, Mr. Zaturecky."

"What do you mean, so much the worse?"

"I think being married is an aggravating circumstance for a womanizer."

"Take that back!" said Mr. Zaturecky menacingly.

"Well, all right," I conceded. "The matrimonial state need not always be an aggravating circumstance. Sometimes it can, on the contrary, excuse a womanizer. But it makes no difference. I've already told you that I'm not angry with you, and I understand you quite well. There's only one thing I don't understand. How can you still want a review from a man whose woman you've been trying to make?"

"Comrade Lecturer! Dr. Kalousek, the editor of the Academy of Sciences journal *Visual Arts* is asking you for this review. And you must write it!"

"The review or the woman. You can't ask for both."

"What kind of behavior is this, comrade?!" screamed Mr. Zaturecky in desperate anger.

The odd thing is that I suddenly felt that Mr. Zaturecky had really wanted to seduce Klara. Seething with rage, I shouted: "You have the audacity to tell me off? You, who should humbly apologize to me in front of my secretary."

I turned my back on Mr. Zaturecky, and, confused, he staggered out.

"Well, then," I sighed with relief, like a general after

the victorious conclusion of a hard campaign, and I said to Marie: "Perhaps he won't want a review by me anymore."

Marie smiled and after a moment timidly asked: "Just why is it that you don't want to write this review?"

"Because, Marie, my dear, what he's written is the most awful crap."

"Then why don't you write in your review that it's crap?"

"Why should I write that? Why do I have to antagonize people?"

Marie was looking at me with an indulgent smile; then the door opened, and there stood Mr. Zaturecky with his arm raised. "It's not me! You're the one who will have to apologize," he shouted in a trembling voice and disappeared again.

7

I don't remember exactly when, perhaps that same day or perhaps a few days later, we found an envelope without an address in my mailbox. Inside was a letter in a clumsy, almost primitive handwriting: "Dear Madame: Present yourself at my house on Sunday regarding the insult to my husband. I shall be at home all day. If you don't present yourself, I shall be forced to take measures. Anna Zaturecky, 14 Dalimilova Street, Prague 3."

Klara was scared and started to say something about my guilt. I waved my hand, declaring that the purpose of life is to give amusement, and if life is too lazy for this, there is nothing left but to help it along a little. Man must constantly saddle events, those swift mares without which he would be dragging his feet in the dust like a weary footslogger. When Klara said that she didn't want to saddle any events, I assured her that she would never meet Mr. or Mrs. Zaturecky, and that I'd take care of the event into whose saddle I had jumped, with one hand tied behind my back.

In the morning, when we were leaving the house, the porter stopped us. The porter wasn't an enemy. Prudently I had once bribed him with a fifty-crown bill, and I had lived until this time in the agreeable conviction that he'd learned not to know anything about me, and didn't add fuel to the fire that my enemies in the house kept blazing.

19

"Some couple was here looking for you yesterday," he said.

"What sort of couple?"

"A little guy with a woman."

"What did the woman look like?"

"Two heads taller than him. Terribly energetic. A stern woman. She was asking about all sorts of things." He turned to Klara. "Mainly about you. Who you are and what your name is."

"Good heavens, what did you say to her?" exclaimed Klara.

"What could I say? How do I know who comes to see the lecturer? I told her that a different woman comes every evening."

"Great!" I laughed and drew a ten-crown note from my pocket. "Just go on talking like that."

"Don't be afraid," I then said to Klara. "You won't go anywhere on Sunday, and nobody will find you."

And Sunday came, and after Sunday, Monday, Tuesday, Wednesday; nothing happened. "You see," I said to Klara.

But then came Thursday. I was telling my students at my customary secret lecture about how feverishly and in what an atmosphere of unselfish camaraderie the young fauvists had liberated color from its former impressionistic character, when Marie opened the door and whispered to me, "The wife of that Zaturecky is here." "But I'm not here," I said. "Just show her the schedule!" But Marie shook her head. "I showed her, but she peeped into your office and saw your raincoat on the stand. So now she's sitting in the corridor waiting."

A blind alley is the place for my best inspirations. I said to my favorite student: "Be so kind as to do me a small favor. Run to my office, put on my raincoat, and go out of the building in it. Some woman will try to prove that you are me, and your task will be not to admit it at any price."

The student went off and returned in about a quarter of an hour. He told me that the mission had been accomplished, the coast was clear, and the woman was out of the building.

This time then I had won.

But then came Friday, and in the afternoon Klara returned from work trembling almost like a leaf.

The polite gentleman who received customers in the tidy office of the dressmaking establishment had suddenly opened the door leading to the workshop, where Klara and fifteen other seamstresses were sitting over their sewing machines, and cried: "Does any one of you live at 5 Zamecka Street?"

Klara knew that it concerned her, because 5 Zamecka Street was my address. However, well-advised caution kept her quiet, for she knew that her living with me was a secret and that nobody knew anything about it.

"You see, that's what I've been telling her," said the polished gentleman when none of the seamstresses spoke up, and he went out again. Klara learned later that a strict female voice on the telephone had made him search through the directory of employees, and had talked for a quarter of an hour trying to convince him that one of the women must live at 5 Zamecka Street.

The shadow of Mrs. Zaturecky was cast over our idyllic room.

"But how could she have found out where you work? After all, here in the house nobody knows about you!" I yelled.

Yes, I was really convinced that nobody knew about us. I lived like an eccentric who thinks that he lives unobserved behind a high wall, while all the time one detail escapes him: The wall is made of transparent glass.

I had bribed the porter not to reveal that Klara lived with me; I had forced Klara into the most troublesome inconspicuousness and concealment and, meanwhile, the whole house knew about her. It was enough that once she had entered into an imprudent conversation with a woman on the second floor—and they got to know where Klara worked.

Without suspecting it we had been living exposed for quite some time. What remained concealed from our persecutors was merely Klara's name. This was the final and only secret behind which, for the time being, we eluded Mrs. Zaturecky, who launched her attack so consistently and methodically that I was horror-struck.

I understood that it was going to be tough. The horse of my story was damnably saddled.

8

This was on Friday. And when Klara came back from work on Saturday, she was trembling again. Here is what had happened:

Mrs. Zaturecky had set out with her husband for the dressmaking establishment. She had called beforehand and asked the manager to allow her and her husband to visit the workshop, to look at the faces of the seamstresses. It's true that this request astonished the Comrade Manager, but Mrs. Zaturecky put on such an air that it was impossible to refuse. She said something vague about an insult, about a ruined existence, and about court. Mr. Zaturecky stood beside her, frowned, and was silent.

They were shown into the workshop. The seamstresses raised their heads indifferently, and Klara recognized the little man; she turned pale and with conspicuous inconspicuousness quickly went on with her sewing.

"Here you are," exclaimed the manager with ironic politeness to the stiff-looking pair. Mrs. Zaturecky realized that she must take the initiative and she urged her husband: "Well, look!" Mr. Zaturecky assumed a scowl and looked around. "Is it one of them?" whispered Mrs. Zaturecky.

Even with his glasses Mr. Zaturecky couldn't see clearly enough to examine the large room, which in any case wasn't easy to survey, filled as it was with piled-up junk, dresses hanging from long horizontal bars, and fidgety seamstresses, who didn't sit neatly with their faces toward the door, but in various positions; they were turning around, getting up and sitting down, and involuntarily averting their faces. Therefore, Mr. Zaturecky had to step forward and try not to skip anyone.

When the women understood that they were being examined by someone, and in addition by someone so unsightly and unattractive, they felt vaguely insulted, and sneers and grumbling began to be heard. One of them, a robust young girl, impertinently burst out: "He's searching all over Prague for the shrew who made him pregnant!"

The noisy, ribald mockery of the women overwhelmed the couple, who stood there timidly with a strange, obstinate dignity.

"Mama," the impertinent girl yelled again at Mrs. Zaturecky, "you don't know how to take care of your little boy! I'd never let such a pretty kid out of the house!"

"Look some more," she whispered to her husband, and sullenly and timidly he went forward step by step as if he were running a gauntlet, but firmly all the same—and he didn't miss a face.

All the time the manager was smiling noncommittally; he knew his women and he knew that you couldn't do anything with them; and so he pretended not to hear their clamor, and he asked Mr. Zaturecky: "Now please tell me what did this woman look like?"

Mr. Zaturecky turned to the manager and spoke

slowly and seriously: "She was beautiful. . . . She was very beautiful."

Meanwhile Klara crouched in a corner, setting herself off from all the playful women by her agitation, her bent head, and her dogged activity. Oh, how badly she feigned her inconspicuousness and insignificance! And Mr. Zaturecky was now close to her; in a moment he would be looking right at her!

"That isn't much, remembering only that she was beautiful," said the polite manager to Mr. Zaturecky. "There are many beautiful women. Was she short or tall?"

"Tall," said Mr. Zaturecky.

"Was she brunette or blonde?" Mr. Zaturecky thought a moment and said: "She was blonde."

This part of the story could serve as a parable on the power of beauty. When Mr. Zaturecky had seen Klara for the first time at my place, he was so dazzled that he actually hadn't seen her. Beauty created an opaque screen before her. A screen of light, behind which she was hidden as if behind a veil.

For Klara is neither tall nor blonde. Only the inner greatness of beauty lent her in Mr. Zaturecky's eyes a semblance of great physical size. And the glow that emanates from beauty lent her hair the appearance of gold.

And so when the little man finally approached the corner where Klara, in a brown work smock, was huddled over a shirt, he didn't recognize her, because he had never seen her.

9

When Klara had finished an incoherent and barely intelligible account of this event I said, "You see, we're lucky."

But amid sobs Klara said to me: "What kind of luck? If they didn't find me today, they'll find me tomorrow."

"I'd like to know how."

"They'll come here for me, to your place."

"I won't let anyone in."

"And what if they send the police?"

"Come on, I'll make a joke of it. After all, it was just a joke and fun."

"These days there's no time for jokes; these days everything is serious. They'll say I wanted to blacken his reputation. When they take a look at him, how could they ever believe that he's capable of trying to seduce a woman?"

"You're right, Klara," I said. "They'll probably lock you up."

"Stop teasing," said Klara. "You know it looks bad for me. I'll have to go before the disciplinary committee and I'll have it on my record and I'll never get out of the workshop; anyway, I'd like to know what's happening about the modeling job you promised me; I can't sleep at your place anymore; I'll always be afraid they're coming for me; today I'm going back to Celakovice."

This was the first conversation of the day.

And that afternoon after a departmental meeting I had a second.

The chairman of the department, a gray-haired art historian and a wise man, invited me into his office.

"I hope you know that you haven't helped yourself with that study essay you've just published," he said to me.

"Yes, I know," I replied.

"Many of our professors think it applies to them, and the dean thinks it was an attack on his views."

"What can be done about it?" I said.

"Nothing," replied the professor, "but your three-year period as a lecturer has expired, and candidates will compete to fill the position. It's customary for the committee to give the position to someone who has already taught in the faculty, but are you so sure that this custom will be upheld in your case? But that isn't what I wanted to talk about. So far it has been in your favor that you lecture regularly, that you're popular with the students, and that you've taught them something. But now you can no longer rely on this. The dean has informed me that for the last three months you haven't lectured at all. And without any excuse. Well, that in itself would be enough for immediate dismissal."

I explained to the professor that I hadn't missed a single lecture, that it had all been a joke, and I told him the whole story about Mr. Zaturecky and Klara.

"Fine, I believe you," said the professor, "but what does it matter if I believe you? Everyone in the entire faculty says that you don't lecture and don't do anything. It's already been discussed at the union meeting, and yesterday they took the matter to the local committee."

"But why didn't they speak to me about it first?"

"What should they speak to you about? Everything is clear to them. Now they're looking back over your whole past behavior, trying to find connections between your past and your present attitude."

"What can they find bad in my past? You know yourself how much I like my work. I've never shirked. My conscience is clear."

"Every human life has many aspects," said the professor. "The past of each one of us can be just as easily arranged into the biography of a beloved statesman as into that of a criminal. Only look thoroughly at yourself. Nobody is denying that you like your work. But what if it served you above all as an opportunity for escape? You weren't often seen at meetings, and when you did come, for the most part, you were silent. Nobody really knew what you thought. I myself remember that several times when a serious matter was being discussed you suddenly made a joke, which caused embarrassment. This embarrassment was of course immediately forgotten, but now, when it is retrieved from the past, it acquires a particular significance. Or remember how various women came looking for you at the university and how you refused to see them. Or else your most recent essay, which anyone who wishes can allege was written from suspicious premises. All these, of course, are isolated facts; but just look at them in the light of your present offense, and they suddenly unite into a totality of significant testimony about your character and attitude."

"But what sort of offense! I'll explain publicly what happened. If people are human they'll have to laugh."

"As you like. But you'll learn either that people aren't human or that you don't know what humans are like. They won't laugh. If you put before them every-thing as it happened, it will then appear that not only did you fail to fulfill your obligations as they were indi-cated on the schedule—that you did not do what you should have done—but on top of this, you lectured secretly—that is, you did what you shouldn't have done. It will appear that you insulted a man who was asking for your help. It will appear that your private life is not in order, that you have some unregistered girl living with you, which will make a very unfavorable impression on the female chairman of the union. The issue will become confused, and God knows what fur-ther rumors will arise. Whatever they are they will cer-tainly be useful to those who have been provoked by your views but were ashamed to be against you because of them."

I knew that the professor wasn't trying to alarm or deceive me. In this matter, however, I considered him a crank and didn't want to give myself up to his skepti-cism. The scandal with Mr. Zaturecky made me go cold all over, but it hadn't tired me out yet. For I had saddled this horse myself, so I couldn't let it tear the reins from my hands and carry me off wherever it wished. I was prepared to engage in a contest with it.

And the horse did not avoid the contest. When I reached home, there in the mailbox was a summons to a meeting of the local committee.

10

The local committee, which was in session in what had been a store, was seated around a long table. The members assumed a gloomy expression when I came in. A grizzled man with glasses and a receding chin pointed to a chair. I said thank you, sat down, and this man took the floor. He informed me that the local committee had been watching me for some time, that it knew very well that I led an irregular private life; that this did not produce a good impression in my neighborhood; that the tenants in my apartment house had already complained about me once, when they couldn't sleep because of the uproar in my apartment; that all this was enough for the local committee to have formed a proper conception of me. And now, on top of all this, Comrade Mrs. Zaturecky, the wife of a scholar, had turned to them for help. Six months ago I should have written a review of her husband's scholarly work, and I hadn't done so, even though I well knew that the fate of the said work depended on my review.

"What do you mean by scientific work?" I interrupted the man with the little chin. "It's a patchwork of plagiarized thoughts."

"That is interesting, comrade." A fashionably dressed blonde of about thirty now joined the discussion; on her face a beaming smile was permanently glued. "Permit me a question: What is your field?"

"I am an art historian."

"And Comrade Zaturecky?"

"I don't know. Perhaps he's trying something similar."

"You see," the blonde turned enthusiastically to the other members, "Comrade Lecturer sees a worker in the same field as a competitor and not as a comrade. This is the way almost all our intellectuals think these days."

"I shall continue," said the man with the receding chin. "Comrade Mrs. Zaturecky told us that her husband visited your apartment and met a woman there. It is said that this woman accused Mr. Zaturecky of wanting to molest her sexually. Comrade Mrs. Zaturecky has in her hand documents that prove her husband is not capable of such a thing. She wants to know the name of this woman who accused her husband, and to transfer the matter to the disciplinary section of the people's committee, because she claims this false accusation has damaged her husband's good name."

I tried again to cut this ridiculous affair short. "Look here, comrades," I said, "it isn't worth all the trouble.

The work in question is so weak that no one else could recommend it either. And if some misunderstanding occurred between this woman and Mr. Zaturecky, it shouldn't really be necessary to call a meeting."

"Fortunately, it is not up to you to decide about our meetings, comrade," replied the man with the receding chin. "And when you now assert that Comrade Zaturecky's work is bad, then we must look upon this as revenge. Comrade Mrs. Zaturecky gave us a letter to read, which you wrote after reading her husband's work."

"Yes. Only in that letter I didn't say a word about what the work is like."

"That is true. But you did write that you would be glad to help him; in this letter it is clearly implied that you respect Comrade Zaturecky's work. And now you declare that it's a patchwork. Why didn't you say it to his face?"

"Comrade Lecturer has two faces," said the blonde.

At this moment an elderly woman with a permanent joined the discussion; she went at once to the heart of the matter. "We would need to know, comrade, who this woman is whom Mr. Zaturecky met at your home."

I understood unmistakably that it wasn't within my power to remove the senseless gravity from the whole affair, and that I could dispose of it in only one way: to blur the traces, to lure them away from Klara, to lead them away from her as the partridge leads the hound away from its nest, offering its own body for the sake of its young.

"Unfortunately I don't remember her name," I said.

"How is it that you don't remember the name of the woman you live with?" questioned the woman with the permanent.

"Comrade Lecturer, you have an exemplary relationship with women," said the blonde.

"Perhaps I could remember, but I'd have to think about it. Do you know when it was that Mr. Zaturecky visited me?"

"That was . . . wait a moment," the man with the receding chin looked at his papers, "the fourteenth, on Wednesday afternoon."

"On Wednesday . . . the fourteenth . . . wait . . ." I held my head in my hand and did some thinking. "Oh, I remember. That was Helena." I saw that they were all hanging expectantly on my words.

"Helena who?"

"Who? I'm sorry, I don't know. I didn't want to ask her that. As a matter of fact, speaking frankly, I'm not even sure that her name is Helena. I only called her that because her husband is red-haired like Menelaus. But anyway, she very much liked being called that. On Tuesday evening I met her in a wineshop and managed to talk to her for a while, when her Menelaus went to the bar to drink a cognac. The next day she came to my place and was there the whole afternoon. Only I had to leave her in the evening for a couple of hours, I had a meeting at the university. When I returned she was disgusted because some little man had molested her and she thought that I had put him up to it. She took offense and didn't want to know me anymore. And so, you see, I didn't even manage to learn her correct name."

"Comrade Lecturer, whether you are telling the truth or not," the blonde went on, "it seems to me to be absolutely incomprehensible that a man like you can educate our youth. Does our life really inspire in you nothing but the desire to carouse and abuse women? Be assured, we shall transmit our opinion about this to the proper places."

"The porter didn't speak about any Helena," broke in the elderly woman with the permanent, "but he did inform us that some unregistered girl from the dress-making establishment has been living with you for a month. Don't forget, comrade, that you are in lodgings. How can you imagine that someone can live with you like this? Do you think that your house is a brothel?"

There flashed before my eyes the ten crowns I'd given the porter a couple of days ago, and I understood that the encirclement was complete. And the woman from the local committee continued: "If you don't want to tell us her name, the police will find it out."

11

The ground was slipping away beneath my feet. At the university I began to sense the malicious atmosphere the professor had told me about. For the time being I wasn't summoned for questioning again, but here and there I caught an allusion, and now and then Marie let something out, for the teachers drank coffee in her office and didn't watch their tongues. In a couple of days the selection committee, which was collecting evidence on all sides, was to meet. I imagined that its members had read the report of the local committee, a report about which I knew only that it was secret and that I couldn't refer to it.

There are moments in life when a man retreats defensively, when he must give ground, when he must surrender less important positions in order to protect the more important ones. It seemed to me that this single, most important position was my love. Yes, in those troubled days I suddenly began to realize that I loved my fragile and unfortunate seamstress, that I really loved her.

That day I met Klara in a church. No, not at home. Do you think that home was still home? Is home a room with glass walls? A room observed through binoculars? A room where you must keep your beloved more carefully hidden than contraband?

Home was not home. There we felt like housebreakers who might be caught at any minute; footsteps in the corridor made us nervous; we kept expecting someone to start pounding on the door. Klara was commuting from Celakovice and we didn't feel like meeting in our alienated home for even a short while. So I had asked an artist friend to lend me his studio at night. That day I had the key for the first time.

And so we found ourselves beneath a high roof, in an enormous room with one small couch and a huge, slanting window, from which we could see all the lights of Prague; amid the many paintings propped against the walls, the untidiness, and the carefree artist's squalor, a blessed feeling of freedom returned to me. I sprawled on the couch, pushed in the corkscrew, and opened a bottle of wine. I chattered gaily and freely, and was looking forward to a beautiful evening and night.

However, the pressure, which I no longer felt, had fallen with its full weight on Klara.

I have already mentioned that Klara without any scruples and with the greatest naturalness had lived at one time in my attic. But now, when we found ourselves for a short time in someone else's studio, she felt put out. More than put out: "It's humiliating," she said.

"What's humiliating?" I asked her.

"That we have to borrow an apartment."

"Why is it humiliating that we have to borrow an apartment?"

"Because there's something humiliating about it," she replied.

"But we couldn't do anything else."

"I guess so," she replied, "but in a borrowed apartment I feel like a whore."

"Good God, why should you feel like a whore in a borrowed apartment? Whores mostly operate in their own apartments, not in borrowed ones."

It was futile to attack with reason the stout wall of irrational feelings that, as is known, is the stuff of which the female soul is made. From the beginning our conversation was ill-omened.

I told Klara what the professor had said, I told her what had happened at the local committee, and I was trying to convince her that in the end we would win if we loved each other and were together.

Klara was silent for a while, and then she said that I myself was responsible for everything.

"Will you at least help me get away from those seamstresses?"

I told her that this would have to be, at least temporarily, a time of forbearance.

"You see," said Klara, "you promised, and in the end you do nothing. I won't be able to get out, even if somebody else wants to help me, because my reputation will be ruined because of you."

I gave Klara my word that the incident with Mr. Zaturecky couldn't harm her.

"I also don't understand," said Klara, "why you won't write the review. If you'd write it, then there'd be peace at once."

"It's too late, Klara," I said. "If I write this review they'll say that I'm condemning the work out of revenge and they'll be still more furious."

"And why do you have to condemn it? Write a favorable review!"

"I can't, Klara. This article is thoroughly absurd."

"So what? Why are you being truthful all of a sudden? Wasn't it a lie when you told the little man that they don't think much of you at *Visual Arts*? And wasn't it a lie when you told the little man that he had tried to seduce me? And wasn't it a lie when you invented

37

Helena? When you've told so many lies, what does it matter if you tell one more and praise him in the review? That's the only way you can smooth things out."

"You see, Klara," I said, "you think that a lie is a lie, and it would seem that you're right. But you aren't. I can invent anything, make a fool of someone, carry out hoaxes and practical jokes—and I don't feel like a liar and I don't have a bad conscience. These lies, if you want to call them that, represent me as I really am. With such lies I'm not simulating anything, with such lies I'm in fact speaking the truth. But there are things I can't lie about. There are things I've penetrated, whose meaning I've grasped, that I love and take seriously. I can't joke about these things. If I did I'd humiliate myself. It's impossible, don't ask me to do it, I can't."

We didn't understand each other.

But I really loved Klara, and I was determined to do all I could so that she would have nothing to reproach me for. The following day I wrote a letter to Mrs. Zaturecky, saying that I would expect her in my office the day after tomorrow at two o'clock.

12

True to her terrifying thoroughness, Mrs. Zaturecky knocked precisely at the appointed time. I opened the door and asked her in.

Then I finally saw her. She was a tall woman, very tall with a thin peasant face and pale blue eyes. "Take off your things," I said, and with awkward movements she took off a long, dark coat, narrow at the waist and oddly styled, a coat that God knows why evoked the image of an old military greatcoat.

I didn't want to attack at once; I wanted my adversary to show me her cards first. After Mrs. Zaturecky sat down, I got her to speak by making a remark or two.

"Lecturer," she said in a serious voice, but without any aggressiveness, "you know why I was looking for you. My husband has always respected you very much as a specialist and as a man of character. Everything depended on your review, and you didn't want to do it for him. It took my husband three years to write this article. His life has been harder than yours. He was a teacher, he commuted every day sixty kilometers away from Prague. Last year I forced him to stop that and devote himself to research."

"Mr. Zaturecky isn't employed?" I asked.

"No."

"What does he live on?"

"For the time being I have to work hard myself. This

research, Lecturer, is my husband's passion. If you only knew how much he's studied. If you only knew how many pages he's rewritten. He always says that a real scholar must write three hundred pages so as to keep thirty. And on top of it, this woman. Believe me, Lecturer, I know him; I'm sure he didn't do it, so why did this woman accuse him? I don't believe it. Let her say it before me and before him. I know women, perhaps she likes you very much and you don't care for her. Perhaps she wanted to make you jealous. But you can believe me, Lecturer, my husband would never have dared!"

I was listening to Mrs. Zaturecky, and all at once something strange happened to me: I ceased being aware that this was the woman for whose sake I would have to leave the university, and that this was the woman who caused the tension between me and Klara, and for whose sake I'd wasted so many days in anger and unpleasantness. The connection between her and the incident, in which we'd both played a sad role, suddenly seemed vague, arbitrary, accidental, and not our fault. All at once I understood that it had only been my illusion that we ourselves saddle events and control their course; the truth is that they aren't *our* stories at all, that they are foisted on us from somewhere *outside*; that in no way do they represent us; that we are not to blame for the strange paths they follow; that they are themselves directed from who knows where by who knows what strange forces.

When I looked at Mrs. Zaturecky's eyes it seemed to

me that these eyes couldn't see the consequences of my actions, that these eyes weren't seeing at all, that they were merely swimming in her face; that they were only stuck on.

"Perhaps you're right, Mrs. Zaturecky," I said in a conciliatory tone. "Perhaps my girl didn't speak the truth, but you know how it is when a man's jealous; I believed her and was carried away. That can happen to anyone."

"Yes, certainly," said Mrs. Zaturecky, and it was evident that a weight had been lifted from her heart. "When you yourself see it, it's good. We were afraid that you believed her. This woman could have ruined my husband's whole life. I'm not even speaking about the shadow this casts upon him from the moral point of view. We could handle that. But my husband is relying on your review. The editors assured him that it depended on you. My husband is convinced that if his article were published he would finally be allowed to do scholarly work. I ask you, now that everything has been cleared up, will you write this review for him? And can you do it quickly?"

Now came the moment to avenge myself on everything and appease my rage, only at this moment I didn't feel any rage, and when I spoke it was only because there was no escaping it: "Mrs. Zaturecky, there is some difficulty regarding the review. I shall confess to you how it all happened. I don't like to say unpleasant things to people's faces. This is my weakness. I avoided Mr. Zaturecky, and I thought that he would figure out

41

why I was avoiding him. His paper is weak. It has no scholarly value. Do you believe me?"

"I find it hard to believe. I can't believe you," said Mrs. Zaturecky.

"Above all, this work is not original. Do you understand? A scholar must always arrive at something new; a scholar can't copy what we already know, what others have written."

"My husband definitely didn't copy."

"Mrs. Zaturecky, you've surely read this article—" I wanted to continue, but Mrs. Zaturecky interrupted me: "No, I haven't."

I was surprised. "Read it, then."

"My eyes are bad," said Mrs. Zaturecky. "I haven't read a single line for five years, but I don't need to read to know if my husband's honest or not. That can be recognized in other ways. I know my husband as a mother knows her children, I know everything about him. And I know that what he does is always honest."

I had to undergo worse. I read aloud to Mrs. Zaturecky paragraphs from various authors whose thoughts and formulations Mr. Zaturecky had taken over. It wasn't a question of willful plagiarism, but rather an unconscious submission to those authorities who inspired in Mr. Zaturecky a feeling of sincere and inordinate respect. It was obvious that no serious scholarly journal could publish Mr. Zaturecky's work.

I don't know how much Mrs. Zaturecky concentrated on my exposition, how much of it she followed and understood; she sat humbly in the armchair, humbly and obediently like a soldier who knows that he may not leave his post. It took about half an hour for us to finish. Mrs. Zaturecky got up from the armchair, fixed her transparent eyes upon me, and in a dull voice begged my pardon; but I knew that she hadn't lost faith in her husband and she didn't reproach anyone except herself for not knowing how to resist my arguments, which seemed obscure and unintelligible to her. She put on her military greatcoat, and I understood that this woman was a soldier in body and spirit, a sad and loyal soldier, a soldier tired from long marches, a soldier who doesn't understand the sense of an order and yet carries it out without objections, a soldier who goes away defeated but without dishonor.

13

"So now you don't have to be afraid of anything," I said to Klara, when later in the Dalmatia Tavern I repeated to her my conversation with Mrs. Zaturecky.

"I didn't have anything to fear anyhow," replied Klara with a self-assurance that astonished me.

"What do you mean, you didn't? If it weren't for you I wouldn't have met with Mrs. Zaturecky at all."

"It's good that you did meet with her, because what you did to them was unnecessary. Dr. Kalousek said that it's hard for a sensible man to understand it."

"When did you see Kalousek?"

"I saw him," said Klara.

"And did you tell him everything?"

"What? Is it a secret, perhaps? Now I know exactly what you are."

"Really?"

"May I tell you what you are?"

"Please."

"A stereotypical cynic."

"You got that from Kalousek."

"Why from Kalousek? Do you think that I can't figure it out for myself? You actually think I'm not capable of forming an opinion about you. You like to lead people by the nose. You promised Mr. Zaturecky a review."

"I didn't promise him a review."

"And you promised me a job. You used me as an excuse to Mr. Zaturecky, and you used Mr. Zaturecky as an excuse to me. But you may be sure that I'll get that job."

"Through Kalousek?" I tried to be scornful.

"Certainly not through you! You've gambled so much away, and you don't even know yourself how much."

"And do you know?"

"Yes. Your contract won't be renewed, and you'll be glad if they'll let you into some little provincial gallery as a clerk. But you must realize that all this was only your own mistake. If I can give you some advice:

44

another time be honest and don't lie, because a man who lies can't be respected by any woman."

She got up, gave me (clearly for the last time) her hand, turned, and left.

Only after a while did it occur to me (in spite of the chilly silence that surrounded me) that my story was not of the tragic sort, but rather of the comic variety.

That afforded me some comfort.

The Golden Apple of Eternal Desire

*. . . they do not know that they seek only
the chase and not the quarry.*

—Blaise Pascal

Martin

Martin is able to do something I'm incapable of. Stop any woman on any street. I must say that during the long time I've known him I've greatly profited from this skill of his, for I like women as much as he does, but I wasn't granted his reckless audacity. On the other hand, Martin committed the error of reducing accosting to an exercise of virtuosity as an end in itself. And so he used to say, not without a certain bitterness, that he was like a soccer forward who unselfishly passes unstoppable balls to his teammate, who then kicks easy goals and reaps cheap glory.

Last Monday afternoon after work I was waiting for him in a café on Vaclav Square, looking through a thick German book on Etruscan culture. It had taken several months for the university library to negotiate its loan from Germany, and now that it had finally come just that day, I carried it off as if it were a relic, and I was actually quite pleased that Martin had kept me waiting, and that I could leaf through the book I'd long wanted at a café table.

Whenever I think about ancient cultures nostalgia seizes me. Perhaps this is nothing but envy of the sweet slowness of the history of that time. The era of ancient

Egyptian culture lasted for several thousand years; the era of Greek antiquity for almost a thousand. In this respect, a single human life imitates the history of mankind; at first it is plunged into immobile slowness, and then only gradually does it accelerate more and more. Just two months ago Martin had turned forty.

The Adventure Begins

It was he who disturbed my thoughtful mood. He appeared suddenly at the glass door of the café and headed for me, making expressive gestures and grimaces in the direction of a table at which a woman was sitting over a cup of coffee. Without taking his eyes off her, he sat down beside me and said: "What do you say about that?"

I felt humiliated; I'd actually been so engrossed in my thick volume that only now did I notice the girl; I had to admit that she was pretty. And at that moment the girl straightened up and called the man with the black bow tie, saying that she wished to pay.

"Pay too!" Martin ordered me.

We thought that we would have to run after the girl, but luckily she was detained at the cloakroom. She had left a shopping bag there, and the cloakroom attendant had to hunt for a while before placing it on the counter in front of the girl. As the girl gave the cloakroom attendant some coins, Martin snatched the German book out of my hands.

"It will be better to put it in here," he said with daredevil nonchalance, and slipped the book carefully into the girl's bag. The girl looked surprised, but she didn't know what she was supposed to say.

"It's uncomfortable to carry in one's hand," continued Martin, and when the girl went to pick up the bag herself, he told me off for not knowing how to behave.

The young woman was a nurse in a country hospital. She was in Prague, she said, only for a look around and was hurrying off to the bus terminal. The short distance to the streetcar stop was enough for us to say everything essential and to agree that on Saturday we would come to the town of B. to visit this lovely young woman, who, as Martin meaningfully pointed out, would certainly have a pretty colleague join us.

The streetcar arrived. I handed the young woman her bag, and she began to take the book out of it, but Martin prevented her with a grand gesture, saying we would come for it on Saturday, and that she should read through it carefully in the meantime. The young woman smiled in a bewildered fashion, the streetcar carried her away, and we waved.

Nothing could be done; the book, which I'd been looking forward to for so long, suddenly found itself in a faraway place; when you came to think of it it was quite annoying; but nonetheless a certain lunacy happily uplifted me on the wings it promptly provided.

Martin immediately began thinking about how to make an excuse for Saturday afternoon and night to his young wife (for this is how things stand: at home he has a young wife; and what is worse, he loves her; and what is still worse, he is afraid of her; and what is far worse still, he is anxious about her).

A Successful Sighting

For our excursion I borrowed a neat little Fiat, and on Saturday at two o'clock I drove up in front of Martin's apartment building; Martin was waiting for me and we set off. It was July and oppressively hot.

We wanted to get to B. as soon as possible, but when we saw, in a village through which we were driving, two young men only in swim trunks and with eloquently wet hair, I stopped the car. The lake was actually not far away, a few paces, a mere stone's throw. I needed to be refreshed; Martin was also for swimming.

We changed into our swim trunks and leaped into the water. I swam quickly to the other side. Martin, however, barely took a dip, washed himself off, and came out again. When I'd had a good swim and returned to shore, I caught sight of him in a state of intent absorption. On the shore a crowd of kids was yelling, somewhere farther off the local young people were playing soccer, but Martin was staring at the sturdy little figure of a young girl, who was perhaps fifteen meters away with her back toward us. Totally motionless, she was observing the water.

"Look," said Martin.

"I am looking."

"And what do you say?"

"What should I say?"

"You don't know what you should say about that?"

"We'll have to wait until she turns around," I suggested.

"Not at all. We don't have to wait until she turns around. What's showing from this side is quite enough for me."

"Okay. But we don't have the time to spend with her."

"A sighting, a sighting," said Martin, and turned to a little boy a short distance away who was putting on his swim trunks: "Say, kid, do you know the name of that girl over there?" and he pointed to the girl, who, apparently in some curious state of apathy, went on standing in the same position.

"That one there?"

"Yes, that one there."

"That one isn't from around here," said the little boy.

Martin turned to a little girl of about twelve, who was sunbathing close by.

"Say, kid, do you know who that girl over there is, the one standing at the edge of the water?"

The little girl obediently sat up. "That one there?"

"Yes, that one."

"That's Marie—"

"Marie? Marie who?"

"Marie Panek, from Traplice."

And the girl still stood with her back to us, looking at the water. Now she bent down for her bathing cap, and when she straightened up again, putting it on her head as she did so, Martin was already at my side saying: "That's Marie Panek from Traplice. Now we can drive on."

He was completely calmed and satisfied, and obviously no longer thinking of anything but the rest of the journey.

A Little Theory

That's what Martin calls *sighting*. From his vast experience, he has come to the conclusion that it is not as difficult, for someone with high numerical requirements, to *seduce* a girl as it is to *know* enough girls one hasn't yet seduced.

Therefore he asserts that it is necessary always, no matter where, and at every opportunity, systematically to sight women, that is, to record in a notebook or in our memories the names of women who have attracted us and whom we could one day *board*.

Boarding is a higher level of activity and means that we will get in touch with a particular woman, make her acquaintance, and gain access to her.

He who likes to look back boastfully will stress the names of the women he's made love to; but he who looks forward, toward the future, must above all see to it that he has plenty of women *sighted* and *boarded.*

Over and above boarding there exists only one last level of activity, and I am happy to point out, in deference to Martin, that those who do not go after anything but this last level are wretched, primitive men, who remind me of village soccer players pressing forward thoughtlessly toward the other team's goal, forgetting that it is not enough to score a goal (and many goals) out of the frenetic desire of the kicker, but that it is first necessary to play a conscientious and systematic game on the field.

"Do you think you'll go look her up in Traplice sometime?" I asked Martin, when we were driving again.

"You never know," said Martin.

Then I said: "In any case the day is beginning propitiously for us."

Game and Necessity

We arrived at the hospital in B. in excellent spirits. It was about three-thirty. We called our nurse on the phone in the lobby. Before long she came down in her cap and white uniform; I noticed that she was blushing, and I took this to be a good sign.

Martin began to talk right away, and the girl informed us that she finished work at seven and that we should wait for her at that time in front of the hospital.

"Have you already arranged it with your girlfriend?" asked Martin, and the girl nodded.

"Yes, we'll both be there."

"Fine," said Martin, "but we can't confront my colleague here with a fait accompli."

"Okay," said the girl, "we can drop in on her; she's in the surgery ward."

As we walked slowly across the hospital courtyard I shyly said: "I wonder if you still have that thick book?"

The nurse nodded, saying that she did, and in fact it was right here at the hospital. A weight fell from my heart, and I insisted that we had to get it first.

Of course it seemed improper to Martin that I should openly give preference to a book over a woman about to be presented to me, but I just couldn't help it. I confess that I had suffered greatly during those few days that the book on Etruscan culture was out of my sight. And it was only through great self-restraint that I had stoically put up with this, not wishing under any circumstances to spoil the Game, whose value I've learned to respect since my youth and to which I now subordinate all my personal interests and desires.

While I was having a touching reunion with my book, Martin continued his conversation with the pretty nurse, and got as far as getting her to promise that she would borrow a cabin at nearby Lake Hoter from a colleague for the evening. We were all perfectly happy. Finally we went across the hospital courtyard to a small green building, where the surgery ward was.

Just then a nurse and a doctor came walking toward us. The doctor was a funny-looking beanpole with protruding ears, which fascinated me all the more because at this moment our nurse elbowed me: I let out a short laugh. When they had passed us Martin turned to me: "You're in luck, my boy. You don't deserve such a gorgeous young woman."

I was ashamed to say that I had only looked at the beanpole, so I simulated approbation. After all, there wasn't any hypocrisy on my part. That is to say I trust Martin's taste more than my own, because I believe that his taste is supported by a much greater *interest* than mine. I like objectivity and order in everything, even in love affairs, and consequently I have more respect for the opinion of a connoisseur than for that of a dilettante.

Someone might consider it hypocritical for me to call myself a dilettante—I, a divorced man who is right now relating one of his (obviously in no way exceptional) affairs. But still I am a dilettante. It could be said that I am *playing* at something that Martin *lives*. Sometimes

I have the feeling that the whole of my polygamous life is a consequence of nothing but my imitation of other men; although I am not denying that I have taken a liking for this imitation. But I cannot rid myself of the feeling that in this liking there remains, all the same, something entirely free, playful, and revocable, something that characterizes visits to art galleries or foreign countries, something not submitted to the unconditional imperative I have suspected behind Martin's erotic life. It is precisely the presence of this unconditional imperative that has raised Martin in my eyes. His judgment about a woman seems to me to be that of Nature herself, Necessity herself speaking through his lips.

Home Sweet Home

When we found ourselves outside the hospital Martin pointed out that everything was going tremendously well for us, and then he added: "Of course we'll have to hurry this evening. I want to be home by nine."

I was amazed: "By nine? That means we'll have to leave here at eight. But then we came here for no reason! I counted on having the whole night!"

"Why do you want us to waste our time?"

"But what sense is there in driving here for one hour? What can you do between seven and eight?"

"Everything. As you noticed, I got hold of the cabin, so that everything will go swimmingly. It will depend only on you, you'll have to show that you're sufficiently determined."

"But why, I ask, must you be home at nine?"

"I promised Jirinka. She's used to playing a game of rummy before going to bed on Saturdays."

"Oh, God . . ." I sighed.

"Yesterday Jirinka had a bad time at the office again, so I should give her this little bit of joy on Saturday, shouldn't I? You know, she's the best woman I've ever had. After all," he added, "you should be pleased anyway that you'll still have the whole night before you in Prague."

I understood that it was useless to object. Martin's misgivings about his wife's peace of mind could never be appeased, and his faith in the endless erotic possibilities of every hour or minute could never be shaken by anything.

"Come," said Martin, "there are still three hours till seven! We won't be idle!"

A Delusion

We started on our way along the broad path of the local park, which served the inhabitants as a promenade. We inspected several pairs of girls who walked by us or were sitting on the benches, but we didn't like the look of them.

Martin, it must be admitted, accosted two of them, entered into conversation with them, and finally arranged a meeting with them, but I knew that he didn't mean it seriously. This was so-called *boarding practice*, which he engaged in from time to time for fear of losing his touch.

Dissatisfied, we went out of the park into the streets, which yawned with small-town vacuity and boredom.

"Let's get something to drink; I'm thirsty," I said to Martin.

We found an establishment above which was the sign CAFÉ. We entered, but inside there was only self-service. It was a tiled room that gave off an air of coldness and hostility. We went over to the counter and bought ourselves watered-down lemonades from a sullen woman, and then carried them over to a table, which, being moist with gravy, invited us to depart hastily.

"Don't worry about it," said Martin. "In our world ugliness has its positive function. No one feels like staying anywhere, people hurry on, and thus arises the desirable pace of life. But we won't let ourselves be provoked by this. We can now talk about all sorts of things in the safety of this ugly place." He drank some lemonade and asked: "Have you boarded that medical student yet?"

"Naturally," I replied.

"And what's she like, then? Describe to me exactly how she looks!"

I described the medical student to him. This was not very difficult for me to do, even though no medical student existed. Yes. Perhaps this puts me in a bad light, but it's like this: *I invented her.*

I give my word that I didn't do it maliciously, neither to show off in front of Martin nor because I wanted to lead him by the nose. I invented the medical student simply because I couldn't resist Martin's insistence.

Martin's claims about my activities were boundless. Martin was convinced that I met new women every day. He saw me as other than I am, and if I had truthfully told him that not only had I not possessed any new women for a week, but hadn't even come close, he would have taken me for a hypocrite.

For this reason a few days earlier I had been forced to dream up my sighting of a medical student. Martin was satisfied, and he urged me to board her. And today he was checking on my progress.

"And about what level is she on? Is she on . . ." He closed his eyes and in the darkness searched for a comparison: Then he remembered a mutual friend: ". . . is she on Marketa's level?"

"She's far better," I said.

"You're kidding," marveled Martin.

"She's on your Jirinka's level."

His own wife was for Martin the supreme criterion. Martin was greatly pleased by my report and fell into a reverie.

A Successful Boarding

Then a girl in corduroy pants and a short jacket walked into the room. She went to the counter, waited for a soda, and took it away to drink. She approached a table adjoining ours, put the glass to her lips, and drank without sitting down.

Martin turned to her: "Miss," he said, "we're strangers here, and we'd like to ask you a question."

The girl smiled. She was rather pretty.

"We're terribly hot, and we don't know what we should do."

"Go swimming!"

"That's just it. We don't know where to go swimming around here."

"There isn't any swimming here."

"How is that possible?"

"There's one swimming pool, but it's been empty for a month now."

"And what about the river?"

"It's being dredged."

"So where do you go swimming?"

"Only at Lake Hoter, but it's at least seven kilometers away."

"That's nothing, we have a car; it would be very nice if you'd accompany us."

"As our guide," I said.

"Our guiding light," Martin corrected me.

"Our starlight," said I.

"Our North Star," said Martin.

"Our planet Venus," I said.

"You're simply our constellation, and you should come with us," said Martin.

The girl was confused by our foolish banter and finally said that she would accompany us, but that she had to take care of something first and then she'd pick up her bathing suit; she said that we should be waiting for her in exactly an hour at this same spot.

We were glad. We watched her as she walked away, cutely swinging her backside and tossing her black curls.

"You see," said Martin, "life is short. We must take advantage of every minute."

In Praise of Friendship

We went once again into the park. Once again we examined several pairs of girls on the benches; it happened that many a young woman was good-looking, but it never happened that her companion was also good-looking.

"In this there is some special law," I said to Martin. "An ugly woman hopes to gain something from the luster of her pretty friend; a pretty woman, for her part, hopes that she will stand out more lustrously against the background of the ugly woman; and for us it follows from this that our friendship is subjected to continuous trials. And it is precisely this that I value, that we will never leave the choice to the random development of events, nor even to some mutual struggle; choice for us is always a matter of courtesy. We offer each other the prettier girl like two old-fashioned gentlemen who can never enter a room because neither wants to be the one who goes first."

"Yes," said Martin with emotion. "You're a true friend. Come, let's go sit down for a while, my legs are aching."

And thus we sat comfortably with our faces turned up toward the face of the sun, and we let the world around us rush on unnoticed.

The Girl in White

Suddenly Martin got up (moved evidently by some mysterious sense) and stared at a secluded path of the park. A girl in a white dress was coming our way. Already from afar, before it was possible to ascertain with complete confidence the proportions of her body or the features of her face, we saw that she possessed unmistakable, special, and very perceptible charm, that there was a certain purity or tenderness in her appearance.

When the girl was fairly close to us, we realized that she was quite young, something between a child and a young woman, and this at once threw us into a state of complete agitation. Martin shot up off the bench: "Miss, I am the director Forman, the film director; you must help us."

He gave her his hand, and the young girl with an utterly astonished expression shook it.

Martin nodded in my direction and said: "This is my cameraman."

"My name is Ondricek," I said, offering my hand.

The girl nodded.

"We're in an awkward situation here. I'm looking for outdoor locations for my film. Our assistant, who knows this area well, was supposed to meet us here, but he hasn't arrived, so that right now we're wondering how to get around in this town and in the surrounding countryside. My friend Ondricek here," joked Martin, "is always studying his fat German book, but unfortunately that is not to be found in there."

The allusion to the book, which I had been deprived of for the whole week, somehow irritated me all of a sudden: "It's a pity that you don't take a greater interest in this book," I attacked my director. "If you prepared thoroughly and didn't leave the studying to your cameramen, maybe your films wouldn't be so superficial and there wouldn't be so much nonsense in them; forgive me." I turned then to the girl with an apology. "Anyhow, we won't bother you with our quarrels about our work; our film will be a historical one about Etruscan culture in Bohemia."

"Yes," the girl nodded.

"It's a rather interesting book—look." I handed the girl the book, and she took it in her hands with a certain religious awe, and when she saw that I wanted her to, she turned the pages lightly.

"Pchacek Castle must surely not be far from here," I continued. "It was the center of the Bohemian Etruscans—but how can we get there?"

"It's only a little way," said the girl, beaming, because her knowledge of the road to Pchacek gave her a little bit of firm ground in the somewhat obscure conversation we were carrying on with her.

"Yes? Do you know the area around there?" asked Martin, feigning great relief.

"Sure I know it," said the girl. "It's an hour away."

"On foot?" asked Martin.

"Yes, on foot," said the girl.

"But luckily we have a car here," I said.

"Wouldn't you like to be our guide?" said Martin, but I didn't continue the customary ritual of witticisms, because I have a more precise sense of psychological judgment than Martin; and I felt that frivolous joking would be more inclined to harm us in this case and that our best weapon was absolute seriousness.

"We don't want, miss, to disturb you in any way," I said, "but if you would be so kind as to devote a short time to us and show us some of the places we're looking for, you would help us a great deal—and we would both be very grateful."

"Certainly," the girl nodded again, "I'll be happy . . . but I . . ." Only now did we notice that she had a shopping bag in her hand and in it two heads of lettuce. "I have to bring Mama the lettuce, but it's not far and I'll be right back."

"Of course you have to take the lettuce to Mama," I said. "We'll wait for you here."

"Yes. It won't take more than ten minutes," said the girl.

Once again she nodded, and then she went off eagerly.

"God!" said Martin.

"First-rate, no?"

"You bet. I'm willing to sacrifice the two nurses for her."

The Insidious Nature of Excessive Faith

But ten minutes passed, a quarter of an hour, and the girl didn't come back.

"Don't be afraid," Martin consoled me. "If anything is certain, then it's this, that she'll come. Our performance was completely plausible, and the girl was in raptures."

I too was of this opinion, and so we went on waiting, with each moment becoming more and more eager for this childish young girl. In the meanwhile, also, the time appointed for our meeting with the girl in corduroy pants went by, but we were so set on our little girl in white that it didn't even occur to us to leave.

And time was passing.

"Listen, Martin, I don't think she's coming back," I said at last.

"How do you explain it? After all, that girl believed in us as in God himself."

"Yes," I said, "and in that lies our misfortune. That is to say she believed us only *too* well!"

"What? Perhaps you'd have wanted her not to believe us?"

"It would perhaps have been better like that. Too much faith is the worst ally." A thought took my fancy; I got really involved in it: "When you believe in something literally, through your faith you'll turn it into something absurd. One who is a genuine adherent, if you like, of some political outlook, never takes its *sophistries* seriously, but only its *practical aims*, which are concealed behind these sophistries. Political rhetoric and sophistries do not exist, after all, in order to be believed; rather, they serve as a common and agreed-upon alibi. Foolish people, who take them seriously, sooner or later discover inconsistencies in them, begin to protest, and finish finally and infamously as heretics and apostates. No, too much faith never brings anything good—and not only to political or religious systems but even to our own system, the one we used to convince the girl."

"Somehow I'm not quite following you anymore."

"It's quite simple: for the girl we were actually two serious and respectable gentlemen, and she, like a well-behaved child who offers her seat to an older person on a streetcar, wanted to please us."

"So why didn't she please us?"

"Because she believed us so completely. She gave Mama the lettuce and at once told her enthusiastically all about us: about the historical film, about the Etruscans in Bohemia, and Mama—"

"Yes, the rest is perfectly clear to me . . ." Martin interrupted me and got up from the bench.

The Betrayal

The sun was already slowly going down over the roofs of the town; it was cooling off a bit, and we felt sad. We went to the café just in case the girl in the corduroy pants was by some mistake still waiting for us. Of course she wasn't there. It was six-thirty. We walked down to the car, and suddenly feeling like two people who had been banished from a foreign city and its pleasures, we said to ourselves that nothing remained for us but to retire to the extraterritorial domain of our own car.

"Come on!" remonstrated Martin in the car. "Anyhow, don't look so gloomy! We don't have any reason for that! The most important thing is still before us!"

I wanted to object that we had no more than an hour for the most important thing, because of Jirinka and her rummy game—but I chose to keep silent.

"Anyway," continued Martin, "it was a fruitful day; the sighting of that girl from Traplice, boarding the girl in the corduroy pants; after all, we have it all set up whenever we feel like it. We don't have to do anything but drive here again!"

I didn't object at all. Sighting and boarding had been excellently brought off. That was quite in order. But at this moment it occurred to me that for the last year, apart from countless sightings and boardings, Martin had not come by anything more worthwhile.

I looked at him. As always his eyes shone with a lust-

70

ful glow. I felt at that moment that I liked Martin and that I also liked the banner under which he had been marching all his life: the banner of the eternal pursuit of women.

Time was passing, and Martin said: "It's seven o'clock."

We drove to within about ten meters of the hospital gate, so that in the rearview mirror I could safely observe who was coming out.

I was still thinking about that banner. And also about the fact that in this pursuit of women from year to year it had become less a matter of women and much more a matter of the pursuit itself. Assuming that the pursuit is known to be *vain* in advance, it is possible to pursue any number of women and thus to make the pursuit an *absolute pursuit*. Yes: Martin had attained the state of being in absolute pursuit.

We waited five minutes. The girls didn't come.

It didn't put me out in the least. It was a matter of complete indifference to me whether they came or not. Even if they came, could we in a mere hour drive with them to the isolated cabin, become intimate with them, make love to them, and at eight o'clock say goodbye pleasantly and take off? No, at the moment when Martin limited our available time to ending on the stroke of eight, he had shifted the whole thing to the sphere of a self-deluding game.

Ten minutes went by. No one appeared at the gate.

Martin became indignant and almost yelled: "I'll give them five more minutes! I won't wait any longer!"

Martin hasn't been young for quite a while now, I speculated further. He truly loves his wife. As a matter of fact he has the most regular sort of marriage. This is a reality. And yet—above this reality (and simultaneously with it), Martin's youth continues, a restless, gay, and erring youth transformed into a mere game, a game that was no longer in any way up to crossing the line into real life and realizing itself as a fact. And because Martin is the knight obsessed by Necessity, he has transformed his love affairs into the harmlessness of the Game, *without knowing it*; so he continues to put his whole inflamed soul into them.

Okay, I said to myself. Martin is the captive of his self-deception, but what am I? What am I? Why do I assist him in this ridiculous game? Why do I, who know that all of this is a delusion, pretend along with him? Am I not then still more ridiculous than Martin? Why should I now behave as if an erotic adventure lies before me, when I know that at most a single aimless hour with unknown and indifferent girls awaits me?

At that moment in the mirror I caught sight of two young women at the hospital gates. Even from that distance they gave off a glow of powder and rouge. They were strikingly chic, and their delay was obviously connected with their well-made-up appearance. They looked around and headed toward our car.

"Martin, there's nothing to be done." I renounced the girls. "It's been more than fifteen minutes. Let's go." And I put my foot on the gas.

Repentance

We drove out of B. We passed the last little houses and drove into the countryside through fields and woods, toward whose treetops a large sun was sinking.

We were silent.

I thought about Judas Iscariot, about whom a brilliant author relates that he betrayed Jesus just because he *believed* in him infinitely: He couldn't wait for the miracle through which Jesus was to have shown all the Jews his divine power, so he handed him over to his tormentors in order to provoke him at last to action; he betrayed him because he longed to hasten his victory.

Oh, God, I said to myself, I've betrayed Martin from far less noble motives; I betrayed him in fact just because I stopped believing in him (and in the divine power of his womanizing); I am a vile compound of Judas Iscariot and of the man whom they called Doubting Thomas. I felt that as a result of my wrongdoing my sympathy for Martin was growing, and that his banner of the eternal chase (which was to be heard still fluttering above us) was reducing me to tears. I began to reproach myself for my overhasty action.

Shall I be in a position more easily to part with these gestures that signify youth for me? And will there remain for me perhaps something other than to *imitate* them and endeavor to find a small, safe place for this foolish activity within my otherwise sensible life? What does it matter that it's all a futile game? What does it matter that I know it? Will I stop playing the game just because it is futile?

The Golden Apple of Eternal Desire

He was sitting beside me, and little by little his indignation subsided.

"Listen," he said, "is that medical student really first-rate?"

"I'm telling you she's on Jirinka's level."

Martin put further questions to me. I had to describe the medical student to him once again.

Then he said: "Perhaps you could hand her over to me afterward?"

I wanted to appear plausible. "That may be quite difficult. It would bother her that you're my friend. She has firm principles."

"She has firm principles," said Martin sadly, and it was plain that he was upset by this.

I didn't want to upset him.

"Unless I could pretend I don't know you," I said. "Perhaps you could pass yourself off as someone else."

"Fine! Perhaps as Forman, like today."

"She doesn't give a damn about film directors. She prefers athletes."

"Why not?" said Martin, "it's all within the realm of possibility," and we spent some time on this discussion. From moment to moment the plan became clearer, and after a while it dangled before us in the advancing twilight like a beautiful, ripe, shining apple.

Permit me to name this apple, with some pomposity, the Golden Apple of Eternal Desire.

The Hitchhiking Game

1

The needle on the gas gauge suddenly dipped toward empty, and the young driver of the sports car declared that it was maddening how much gas the car guzzled. "See that we don't run out of gas again," protested the girl (about twenty-two), and she reminded the driver of several places where this had already happened to them. The young man replied that he wasn't worried, because whatever he went through with her had the charm of adventure for him. The girl objected; whenever they had run out of gas on the highway it had, she said, always been an adventure only for her. The young man had hidden, and she had had to make ill use of her charms by thumbing a ride and letting herself be driven to the nearest gas station, then thumbing a ride back with a can of gas. The young man asked the girl whether the drivers who had given her a ride had been unpleasant, since she spoke as if her task had been a hardship. She replied (with awkward flirtatiousness) that sometimes they had been very pleasant, but that it hadn't done her any good as she had been burdened with the can and had had to leave them before she could get anything going. "Sex fiend," said the young man. The girl protested that it was he who was the sex fiend. God knows how many girls stopped him on the highway when he was driving the car alone! Still driving, the young man put his arm around the girl's shoulders and kissed her gently on the forehead. He knew that she loved him and that she was jealous. Jealousy isn't a pleasant trait, but if it isn't overdone (and if it's combined with modesty), apart from its inconvenience there's even something touching about it. At least that's what the young man thought. Because he was only twenty-eight, it seemed to him that he was old and knew everything that a man could know about women. In the girl sitting beside him he valued precisely what, until now, he had encountered least in women: purity.

The needle was already on empty when, to the right, the young man caught sight of a sign announcing that a gas station was five hundred meters ahead. The girl hardly had time to say how relieved she was before the young man was signaling left and driving into a space in front of the pumps. However, he had to stop a little way off, because beside the pumps was a huge gasoline truck with a large metal tank and a bulky hose, which was refilling the pumps. "We'll have to wait," said the young man to the girl, and he got out of the car. "How long will it take?" he shouted to the man in overalls. "Only a moment," replied the attendant, and the young man said: "I've heard that one before." He wanted to go back and sit in the car, but he saw that the girl had gotten out the other side. "I'll take a little walk in the meantime," she said. "Where to?" the young man asked on purpose, wanting to see the girl's embarrassment. He had known her for a year now, but she would still blush in front of him. He enjoyed her moments of modesty, partly because they distinguished her from the women he'd met before, partly because he was aware of the law of universal transience, which made even his girl's modesty a precious thing to him.

2

The girl really didn't like it when during a trip (the young man would drive for several hours without stopping) she had to ask him to stop for a moment somewhere near a clump of trees. She always got angry when, with feigned surprise, he asked her why he should stop. She knew that her modesty was ridiculous and old-fashioned. Many times at work she had noticed that they laughed at her on account of it and deliberately provoked her. She always blushed in advance at the idea that she was going to blush. She often longed to feel free and easy about her body, the way most of the women around her did. She had even invented a special course in self-persuasion: she would repeat to herself that at birth every human being received one out of the millions of available bodies, as one would receive an allotted room out of the millions of rooms in an enormous hotel; that consequently the body was fortuitous and impersonal, only a ready-made, borrowed thing. She would repeat this to herself in different ways, but she could never manage to feel it. This mind-body dualism was alien to her. She was too much at one with her body; that is why she always felt such anxiety about it.

She experienced this same anxiety even in her relations with the young man, whom she had known for a year and with whom she was happy, perhaps because he never separated her body from her soul, and she could live with him wholly. In this unity there was happiness, but it is not far from happiness to suspicion, and the girl was full of suspicions. For instance, it often occurred to her that other women (those who weren't anxious) were more attractive and more seductive, and that the young man, who did not conceal the fact that he knew this kind of woman well, would someday leave her for a woman like that. (True, the young man declared that he'd had enough of them to last his whole life, but she knew that he was still much younger than he thought.) She wanted him to be completely hers and herself to be completely his, but it often seemed to her that the more she tried to give him everything, the more she denied him something: the very thing that a light and superficial love or a flirtation gives a person. It worried her that she was not able to combine seriousness with lightheartedness.

But now she wasn't worrying, and any such thoughts were far from her mind. She felt good. It was the first day of their vacation (of their two-week vacation, which she had been dreaming about for a whole year), the sky was blue (the whole year she had been worrying about whether the sky would really be blue), and he was beside her. At his "Where to?" she blushed, and she left the car without a word. She walked around the gas station, which was situated beside the highway in total isolation, surrounded by fields. About a hundred meters away (in the direction in which they were traveling), a wood began. She set off for it, vanished behind a little bush, and gave herself up to her good mood. (In solitude it was possible for her to get the greatest enjoyment from the presence of the man she loved. If his presence had been continuous, it would have kept on disappearing. Only when she was alone was she able to hold on to it.)

When she came out of the wood onto the highway, the gas station was visible. The large gasoline truck was already pulling out, and the sports car moved forward toward the red column of the pump. The girl walked on along the highway and only at times looked back to see if the sports car was coming. At last she caught sight of it. She stopped and began to signal at it like a hitchhiker signaling at a stranger's car. The sports car slowed down and stopped close to the girl. The young man leaned toward the window, rolled it down, smiled, and asked: "Where are you headed, miss?" "Are you going to Bystrica?" asked the girl, smiling flirtatiously at him. "Yes, please get in," said the young man, opening the door. The girl got in, and the car took off.

3

The young man was always glad when his girlfriend was in a good mood. This didn't happen too often; she had quite a tiresome job in an unpleasant environment, many hours of overtime without compensatory leisure, and, at home, a sick mother. So she often felt tired. She didn't have either particularly good nerves or self-confidence, and she fell easily into a state of anxiety and fear. For this reason he welcomed every manifestation of her gaiety with the tender solicitude of an older brother. He smiled at her and said: "I'm lucky today. I've been driving for five years, but I've never given a ride to such a pretty hitchhiker."

The girl was grateful to the young man for every bit of flattery; she wanted to linger for a moment in its warmth, and so she said: "You're very good at lying."

"Do I look like a liar?"

"You look like you enjoy lying to women," said the girl, and into her words there crept unawares a touch of the old anxiety, because she really did believe that her young man enjoyed lying to women.

The girl's jealousy often irritated the young man, but this time he could easily overlook it for, after all, her words didn't apply to him but to an unknown driver. And so he merely asked an ordinary question: "Does it bother you?"

"If I were going out with you, then it would bother me," said the girl and her words contained a subtle, instructive message for the young man; but the end of her sentence applied only to the unknown driver: "but I don't know you, so it doesn't bother me."

"Things about her own man always bother a woman more than things about a stranger" (this was now the young man's subtle, instructive message to the girl), "so seeing that we are strangers, we could get along well together."

The girl pretended not to understand the implied meaning of his message, and so she now addressed the unknown driver exclusively: "What does it matter, since we'll part company in a little while?"

"Why?" asked the young man.

"Well, I'm getting out at Bystrica."

"And what if I get out with you?"

At these words the girl looked up at him and found that he looked exactly as she imagined him in her most agonizing hours of jealousy. She was alarmed at how he was flattering her and flirting with her (an unknown hitchhiker), and how seductive he was. Therefore she responded with defiant provocativeness: "What would *you* do with me, I wonder?"

"I wouldn't have to think too hard about what to do with such a beautiful woman," said the young man gallantly, and at this moment he was once again speaking far more to his own girl than to the figure of the hitchhiker.

But this flattering sentence made the girl feel as if she had caught him at something, as if she had wheedled a confession out of him with a fraudulent trick.

She felt toward him a brief flash of intense hatred and said: "Aren't you rather too sure of yourself?"

The young man looked at the girl. Her defiant face appeared to him to be completely convulsed. He felt sorry for her and longed for her usual, familiar expression (which he considered childish and simple). He leaned toward her, put his arm around her shoulders, and softly spoke the nickname he often used and with which he now wanted to stop the game.

But the girl released herself and said: "You're going a bit too fast!"

At this rebuff the young man said: "Excuse me, miss," and looked silently in front of him at the highway.

4

The girl's pitiful jealousy, however, left her as quickly as it had come over her. After all, she was sensible and knew perfectly well that all this was merely a game; now it even struck her as a little ridiculous that she had repulsed her man out of jealous rage; it wouldn't be pleasant for her if he found out why she had done it. Fortunately she had the miraculous ability to change the meaning of her actions after the event. Using this ability, she decided that she had repulsed him not out of anger but so that she could go on with the game, which, with its whimsicality, so well suited the first day of their vacation.

So again she was the hitchhiker who had just repulsed the overeager driver, but only so as to slow down his conquest and make it more exciting. She half turned toward the young man and said caressingly: "I didn't mean to offend you, mister!"

"Excuse me, I won't touch you again," said the young man.

He was furious with the girl for not listening to him and refusing to be herself when that was what he wanted. And since the girl insisted on continuing in her role, he transferred his anger to the unknown hitchhiker whom she was portraying. And all at once he discovered the character of his own role: he stopped making the gallant remarks with which he had wanted to flatter his girl in a roundabout way, and began to play the tough guy who treats women to the coarser aspects of his masculinity: willfulness, sarcasm, self-assurance.

This role was a complete contradiction of the young man's habitually solicitous approach to the girl. True, before he had met her he had in fact behaved roughly rather than gently toward women. But he had never resembled a heartless tough guy, because he had never demonstrated either a particularly strong will or ruthlessness. However, if he did not resemble such a man, nonetheless he had longed to at one time. Of course it was a quite naive desire, but there it was. Childish desires withstand all the snares of the adult mind and often survive into ripe old age. And this childish desire quickly took advantage of the opportunity to embody itself in the proffered role.

The young man's sarcastic reserve suited the girl very well—it freed her from herself. For she herself was, above all, the epitome of jealousy. The moment she stopped seeing the gallantly seductive young man beside her and saw only his inaccessible face, her jealousy subsided. The girl could forget herself and give herself up to her role.

Her role? What was her role? It was a role out of trashy literature. The hitchhiker stopped the car not to get a ride, but to seduce the man who was driving the car. She was an artful seductress, cleverly knowing how to use her charms. The girl slipped into this silly, romantic part with an ease that astonished her and held her spellbound.

5

There was nothing the young man missed in his life more than lightheartedness. The main road of his life was drawn with implacable precision: his job didn't use up merely eight hours a day, it also infiltrated the remaining time with the compulsory boredom of meetings and home study, and, by means of the attentiveness of his countless male and female colleagues, it infiltrated the wretchedly little time he had left for his private life as well; this private life never remained secret and sometimes even became the subject of gossip and public discussion. Even a two week vacation didn't give him a feeling of liberation and adventure; the gray shadow of precise planning lay even here. The scarcity of summer accommodations in our country had compelled him to book a room in the Tatras six months in advance, and since for that he needed a recommendation from his office, its omnipresent brain thus did not cease knowing about him for even an instant.

He had become reconciled to all this, yet all the same from time to time the terrible thought of the straight road would overcome him—a road along which he was being pursued, where he was visible to everyone, and from which he could not turn aside. At this moment that thought returned to him. Through an odd and brief conjunction of ideas the figurative road became identified with the real highway along which he was driving—and this led him suddenly to do a crazy thing.

"Where did you say you wanted to go?" he asked the girl.

"To Bystrica," she replied.

"And what are you going to do there?"

"I have a date there."

"Who with?"

"With a certain gentleman."

The car was just coming to a large crossroads. The

driver slowed down so as to read the road signs, then turned off to the right.

"What will happen if you don't turn up for that date?"

"I would be your fault, and you would have to take care of me."

"You obviously didn't notice that I turned off in the direction of Nove Zamky."

"Is that true? You've gone crazy!"

"Don't worry! I'll take care of you," said the young man.

The game all at once went into a higher gear. The sports car was moving away not only from the imaginary goal of Bystrica, but also from the real goal, toward which it had been heading in the morning: the Tatras and the room that had been reserved. Fiction was suddenly making an assault on real life. The young man was moving away from himself and from the implacable straight road, from which he had never strayed until now.

"But you said you were going to the Tatras!" The girl was surprised.

"I'm going, miss, wherever I feel like going. I'm a free man, and I do what I want and what it pleases me to do."

6

When they drove into Nove Zamky it was already getting dark.

The young man had never been here before, and it took him a while to orient himself. Several times he stopped the car and asked the passersby directions to the hotel. Several streets had been dug up, so that the drive to the hotel, even though it was quite close by (as all those who had been asked asserted), necessitated so many detours and roundabout routes that it was almost a quarter of an hour before they finally stopped in front of it. The hotel looked unprepossessing, but it was the only one in town and the young man didn't feel like driving on. So he said to the girl: "Wait here," and he got out of the car.

Out of the car he was, of course, himself again. And it was upsetting for him to find himself in the evening somewhere completely different from his intended destination—the more so because no one had forced him to do it and as a matter of fact he hadn't even really wanted to. He blamed himself for this piece of folly, but then became reconciled to it. The room in the Tatras could wait until tomorrow, and it wouldn't do any harm if they celebrated the first day of their vacation with something unexpected.

He walked through the restaurant—smoky, noisy, and crowded—and asked for the reception desk. They sent him to the back of the lobby near the staircase, where behind a glass panel a superannuated blonde was sitting beneath a board full of keys. With difficulty, he obtained the key to the only room left.

The girl, when she found herself alone, also threw off her role. She didn't feel ill-humored, though, at finding herself in an unexpected town. She was so devoted to the young man that she never had doubts about anything he did, and confidently entrusted every moment of her life to him. On the other hand the idea once again popped into her mind that perhaps—just as she was now doing—other women had waited for her man in his car, those women he met on business trips. But surprisingly enough this idea didn't upset her at all now; in fact, she smiled at the thought of how nice it was that today she was this other woman, this irresponsible, indecent other woman, one of those women of whom she was so jealous; it seemed to her that she was cutting them all out, that she had learned how to use their weapons; how to give the young man what until now she had not known how to give him: lightheartedness, shamelessness, and dissoluteness; a curious feeling of satisfaction filled her, because she alone had the ability to be all women and in this way (she alone) could completely captivate her lover and hold his interest.

The young man opened the car door and led the girl into the restaurant. Amid the din, the dirt, and the smoke he found a single unoccupied table in a corner.

7

"So how are you going to take care of me now?" asked the girl provocatively.

"What would you like for an aperitif?"

The girl wasn't too fond of alcohol, still she drank a little wine and liked vermouth fairly well. Now, however, she purposely said: "Vodka."

"Fine," said the young man. "I hope you won't get drunk on me."

"And if I do?" said the girl.

The young man did not reply but called over a waiter and ordered two vodkas and two steak dinners. In a moment the waiter brought a tray with two small glasses and placed it in front of them.

The man raised his glass, "To you!"

"Can't you think of a wittier toast?"

Something was beginning to irritate him about the girl's game; now sitting face-to-face with her, he realized that it wasn't just the *words* that were turning her into a stranger, but that she had *completely* changed, the movements of her body and her facial expression, and that she unpalatably and faithfully resembled a type of woman he knew all too well and inspired some aversion in him.

And so (holding his glass in his raised hand), he corrected his toast: "Okay, then I won't drink to you, but to your kind, in which are combined so successfully the better qualities of the animal and the worse aspects of the human being."

"By 'kind' do you mean all women?" asked the girl.

"No, I mean only those who are like you."

"Anyway, it doesn't seem very witty to me to compare a woman to an animal."

"Okay," the young man was still holding his glass aloft, "then I won't drink to your kind, but to your soul. Agreed? To your soul, which lights up when it descends from your head into your belly, and which goes out when it rises back up to your head."

The girl raised her glass. "Okay, to my soul, which descends into my belly."

"I'll correct myself once more," said the young man. "To your belly, into which your soul descends."

"To my belly," said the girl, and her belly (now that they had named it specifically) seemed to respond to the call; she could feel every bit of its skin.

Then the waiter brought their steaks, and the young man ordered them another vodka and some soda water (this time they drank to the girl's breasts), and the conversation continued in this peculiar, frivolous tone. It irritated the young man more and more to see how well his girlfriend *knew* how to behave like a loose woman; if she was able to do it so well, he thought, it meant that she really was like that; after all, no alien soul had entered into her from somewhere in space; what she was acting now was she herself; perhaps it was that part of her being that had formerly been locked up and that the pretext of the game had let out of its cage. Perhaps the girl supposed that by means of the game she was *disowning* herself, but wasn't it the other way around? Wasn't she becoming herself only through the game? Wasn't she freeing herself through the game? No, sitting opposite him was not a strange woman in his girl's body; it was his girl, herself, no one else. He looked at her and felt growing aversion toward her.

However, it was not only aversion. The more the girl withdrew from him psychically, the more he longed for her physically; the alienation of her soul drew attention to her body; yes it turned her body into a body; as if until now it had been hidden from the young man within clouds of compassion, tenderness, concern, love, and emotion, as if it had been lost in these clouds (yes, as if this body had been *lost*!). It seemed to the young man that today he was *seeing* his girl's body for the first time.

After her third vodka and soda the girl got up and said flirtatiously: "Excuse me."

The young man said, "May I ask you where you are going, miss?"

"To piss, if you'll permit me," said the girl, and she walked off between the tables back toward the plush curtain.

8

She was pleased with the way she had astounded the young man with this word, which—in spite of all its innocence—he had never heard from her; nothing seemed to her truer to the character of the woman she was playing than this flirtatious emphasis placed on the word in question; yes, she was pleased, she was in the best of moods; the game captivated her. It allowed her to what she had not felt until now: *a feeling of happy-go-lucky irresponsibility.*

She who was always uneasy in advance about her every next step, suddenly felt completely relaxed. The alien life in which she had become involved was a life without shame, without biographical specifications, without past or future, without obligations; it was a life that was extraordinarily free. The girl, as a hitchhiker, could do anything: *Everything was permitted her*; she could say, do, and feel whatever she liked.

She walked through the room and was aware that people were watching her from all the tables; it was also a new sensation, one she didn't recognize: *indecent joy caused by her body.* Until now she had never been able to get rid of the fourteen-year-old girl within herself who was ashamed of her breasts and had the disagreeable feeling that she was indecent, because they stuck out from her body and were visible. Even though she was proud of being pretty and having a good figure, this feeling of pride was always immediately curtailed by shame; she rightly suspected that feminine beauty functioned above all as sexual provocation, and she found this distasteful; she longed for her body to relate only to the man she loved; when men stared at her breasts in the street it seemed to her that they were invading a piece of her most secret privacy that should belong only to herself and her lover. But now she was the hitchhiker, the woman without a destiny. In this role she was relieved of the tender bonds of her love and began to be intensely aware of her body; and her body became more aroused the more alien the eyes watching it.

She was walking past the last table when an intoxicated man, wanting to show off his worldliness, addressed her in French: "*Combien, mademoiselle?*"

The girl understood. She thrust out her breasts and fully experienced every movement of her hips, then disappeared behind the curtain.

9

It was a peculiar game. This peculiarity was evidenced, for example, by the fact that the young man, even though he himself was playing the unknown driver remarkably well, did not for a moment stop seeing his girl in the hitchhiker. And it was precisely this that was tormenting; he saw his girl seducing a strange man, and he had the bitter privilege of being present, of seeing at close quarters how she looked and of hearing what she said when she was cheating on him (when she had cheated on him, when she would cheat on him); he had the paradoxical honor of being himself the pretext for her unfaithfulness.

This was all the worse because he worshiped rather than loved her; it had always seemed that the girl had *reality* only within the bounds of fidelity and purity, and that beyond these bounds it simply didn't exist; beyond these bounds she would cease to be herself, as water ceases to be water beyond the boiling point. When he now saw her crossing this horrifying boundary with nonchalant elegance, he was filled with anger.

The girl came back from the rest room and complained: "A guy over there asked me: '*Combien, mademoiselle?*'"

"Don't be surprised!" said the young man. "You look like a whore."

"Do you know that it doesn't bother me in the least?"

"Then you should go with the gentleman!"

"But I have you."

"You can join him later. Go and work out something with him."

"I don't find him attractive."

"But in principle you have nothing against it, having several men in one night."

"Why not? If they're good-looking."

"Do you prefer them one after the other or at the same time?"

"Either way," said the girl.

The conversation was proceeding to still greater enormities; it shocked the girl slightly, but she couldn't protest. Even in a game there lurks a lack of freedom; even a game is a trap for the players. If this had not been a game and they had really been two strangers, the hitchhiker could long ago have taken offense and left; but there's no escape from a game. A team cannot flee before the end of the match, chess pieces cannot desert the chessboard, the boundaries of the playing field are impassable. The girl knew that she had to accept whatever form the game might take, just because it was a game. She knew that the more extreme the game became, the more it would be a game and the more obediently she would have to play it. And it was futile to evoke good sense and warn her dazed soul that she must keep her distance from the game and not take it seriously. Just because it was only a game her soul was not afraid, did not oppose the game, and sank deeper into it as if drugged.

The young man called the waiter and paid. Then he got up and said to the girl: "We're going."

"Where to?" The girl feigned surprise.

"Don't ask, just come on," said the young man.

"Is that any way to talk to me?"

"It's the way I talk to whores."

10

They went up the badly lit staircase. On the landing below the second floor a group of intoxicated men was standing near the rest room. The young man caught hold of the girl from behind so that he was holding her breast with his hand. The men by the rest room saw this and began to call out. The girl wanted to break away, but the young man yelled at her: "Keep still!" The men greeted this with general ribaldry and addressed several dirty remarks to the girl. The young man and the girl reached the second floor. He opened the door of their room and switched on the light.

It was a narrow room with two beds, a small table, a chair, and a washbasin. The young man locked the door and turned to the girl. She was standing facing him in a defiant pose with insolent sensuality in her eyes. He looked at her and tried to discover behind her lascivious expression the familiar features that he loved tenderly. It was as if he were looking at two images through the same lens, at two images superimposed one on the other with one showing through the other. These two images showing through each other were telling him that *everything* was in the girl, that her soul was terrifyingly amorphous, that it held faithfulness and unfaithfulness, treachery and innocence, flirtatiousness and chastity. This disorderly jumble seemed disgusting to him, like the variety to be found in a pile of garbage. Both images continued to show through each other, and the young man understood that the girl differed only on the surface from other women, but deep down was the same as they: full of all possible thoughts, feelings, and vices, which justified all his secret misgivings and fits of jealousy. The impression that certain outlines delineated her as an individual was only a delusion to which the other person, the one who was looking, was subject—namely himself. It seemed to him that the girl he loved was a creation of his desire, his thoughts, and his faith and that the *real* girl now standing in front of him was hopelessly *other*, hopelessly *alien*, hopelessly *polymorphous*. He hated her.

"What are you waiting for? Strip!" he said.

The girl flirtatiously bent her head and said: "Is it necessary?"

The tone in which she said this seemed to him very familiar; it seemed to him that once long ago some other woman had said this to him, only he no longer knew which one. He longed to humiliate her. Not the hitchhiker, but his own girl. The game merged with life. The game of humiliating the hitchhiker became only a pretext for humiliating his girl. The young man had forgotten that he was playing a game. He simply hated the woman standing in front of him. He stared at her and drew a fifty-crown bill from his wallet. He offered it to the girl. "Is that enough?"

The girl took the fifty crowns and said: "You don't think I'm worth much."

The young man said: "You aren't worth more."

The girl nestled up against the young man. "You

can't get around me like that. You have to be nicer. You have to make an effort!"

She put her arms around him and moved her mouth toward his. He put his fingers on her mouth and gently pushed her away. He said: "I only kiss women I love."

"And you don't love me?"

"No."

"Who do you love?"

"What's that got to do with you? Strip!"

11

She had never undressed like this before. The shyness, the feeling of inner panic, the dizziness, all that she had always felt when undressing in front of the young man (and she couldn't hide in the darkness), all this was gone. She was standing in front of him self-confident, insolent, bathed in light, and astonished at her sudden discovery of the gestures, heretofore unknown to her, of a slow, provocative striptease. She took in his glances, slipping off each piece of clothing with a caressing movement and enjoying each individual stage of this exposure.

But then suddenly she was standing in front of him completely naked, and at this moment it flashed through her head that now the whole game would end, that since she had stripped off her clothes, she had also stripped away her dissimulation, and that being naked meant that she was now herself and the young man ought to come up to her now and make a gesture with which he would wipe out everything and after which would follow only their most intimate lovemaking. So she stood naked in front of the young man and at that moment stopped playing the game. She felt embarrassed, and on her face appeared the smile that really belonged to her: a shy and confused smile.

But the young man didn't come to her and didn't end the game. He didn't notice the familiar smile; he saw before him only the beautiful, alien body of his own girl, whom he hated. Hatred cleansed his sensuality of any sentimental coating. She wanted to come to him, but he said: "Stay where you are, I want to have a good look at you." Now he longed only to treat her as a whore. But the young man had never had a whore, and the ideas he had about them came from literature and hearsay. So he turned to these ideas and the first thing he recalled was the image of a woman in black underwear (and black stockings) dancing on the shiny top of a piano. In the little hotel room there was no piano, there was only a small table, covered with a linen cloth, leaning against the wall. He ordered the girl to climb up on it. The girl made a pleading gesture, but the young man said: "You've been paid."

When she saw the look of unshakable obsession in the young man's eyes, she tried to go on with the game, even though she no longer could and no longer knew

103

how. With tears in her eyes she climbed onto the table.
The top was scarcely a yard square and one leg was a
little bit shorter than the others, so that standing on it
the girl felt unsteady.

But the young man was pleased with the naked figure now towering above him, and the girl's ashamed
uncertainty merely inflamed his imperiousness. He
wanted to see her body in all positions and from all
sides, as he imagined other men had seen it and would
see it. He was vulgar and lascivious. He used words she
had never heard from him before. She wanted to
refuse, she wanted to be released from the game. She
called him by his first name, but he immediately yelled
at her that she had no right to address him so inti-
mately. And so eventually in confusion and on the
verge of tears, she obeyed, she bent forward and
crouched according to the young man's wishes, gave a
military salute, and then wiggled her hips as she did
the twist for him; during a slightly more violent movement, when the cloth slipped beneath her feet and she
nearly fell, the young man caught her and dragged her
to the bed.

He had intercourse with her. She was glad that at
least now finally the unfortunate game would end and
they would again be the two people they had been
before and would love each other. She wanted to press
her mouth against his. But the young man pushed her
head away and repeated that he only kissed women he
loved. She burst into loud sobs. But she wasn't even
allowed to cry, because the young man's furious pas-

sion gradually won over her body, which then silenced the complaint of her soul. On the bed there were soon two bodies in perfect harmony, two sensual bodies alien to each other. This was exactly what the girl had most dreaded all her life and had scrupulously avoided until now: lovemaking without emotion or love. She knew that she had crossed the forbidden boundary, but she proceeded across it without objections and as a full participant; only somewhere, far off in a corner of her consciousness, did she feel horror at the thought that she had never known such pleasure, never so much pleasure as at this moment—beyond that boundary.

12

Then it was all over. The young man got up off the girl and, reaching out for the long cord hanging over the bed, switched off the light. He didn't want to see the girl's face. He knew that the game was over, but he didn't feel like returning to their customary relationship; he feared this return. He lay beside the girl in the dark in such a way that their bodies would not touch.

After a moment he heard her sobbing quietly; the girl's hand diffidently, childishly touched his; it touched, withdrew, then touched again, and then a pleading, sobbing voice broke the silence, calling him by his name and saying "I'm me, I'm me. . . ."

The young man was silent, he didn't move, and he was aware of the sad emptiness of the girl's assertion, in which the unknown was defined by the same unknown.

And the girl soon passed from sobbing to loud crying and went on endlessly repeating this pitiful tautology: "I'm me, I'm me, I'm me. . . ."

The young man began to call compassion to his aid (he had to call it from afar, because it was nowhere near at hand), so as to be able to calm the girl. There were still thirteen days of vacation before them.

Symposium

ACT ONE
The Staff Room

The doctors' staff room (in any ward of any hospital in any town you like) has brought together five characters and intertwined their actions and speech into a trivial yet, for all that, most enjoyable story.

Dr. Havel and Nurse Elisabet are here (today both of them are on the night shift), and there are two additional doctors (a less than important pretext led them here, so that they could sit with the two who are on duty over a couple of bottles of wine): the bald chief physician of this ward and a comely thirty-year-old woman doctor from another ward, who the whole hospital knows are going with each other.

(The chief physician is, of course, married, and just a moment before he had uttered his favorite maxim, which should give evidence not only of his wit but also of his intentions: "My dear colleagues, as you know, the greatest misfortune for a man is a happy marriage; he hasn't the slightest hope of a divorce.")

In addition to these four there is still a fifth, but he is not actually here, because, as the youngest, he has just been sent for another bottle. And there is a window here, important because it's open and because through it from the darkness outside there enters into the room a warm, fragrant, and moonlit summer night. And finally, there is an agreeable mood here, manifesting itself in the appreciative chatter of all, especially, however, of the chief physician, who listens to his own adages with enamored ears.

A little later in the evening (and only here in fact does our story begin), certain tensions can be noted: Elisabet has drunk more than is advisable for a nurse on duty, and on top of that, begun to behave toward Havel with defiant flirtatiousness, which goes against the grain with him and provokes him to admonishing invective.

Havel's Admonition

"My dear Elisabet, I don't get you. Every day you rummage around in festering wounds, you jab old men in their wrinkled backsides, you give enemas, you take out bedpans. Your lot has provided you with the enviable opportunity to understand human corporeality in all its metaphysical vanity. But your vitality is incorrigible. It is impossible to shake your tenacious desire to be flesh and nothing but flesh. Your breasts know how to rub against a man standing five meters away from you. My head is already spinning from those eternal gyrations your untiring butt describes when you walk. Go to the devil, get away from me! Those boobs of yours are ubiquitous—like God! You should have given the injections ten minutes ago!"

Dr. Havel Is Like Death; He Takes Everything

When Nurse Elisabet (ostentatiously offended) had left the staff room, condemned to jab two very old backsides, the chief physician said: "I ask you, Havel, why do you insist on turning down poor Elisabet?"

Dr. Havel took a sip of wine and replied: "Chief, don't get mad at me for that. It's not because she isn't pretty and is getting on in years. Believe me, I've had women still uglier and far older."

"Yes, it's a well-known fact about you: you're like death; you take everything. But if you take everything, why don't you take Elisabet?"

"Maybe," said Havel, "it's because she shows her desire so conspicuously that it resembles an order. You say that I am like death in relation to women. But not even death likes to be given an order."

The Chief Physician's Greatest Success

"I think I understand you," the chief physician answered. "When I was some years younger, I knew a girl who went to bed with everyone, and because she was pretty I was determined to have her. And imagine, she turned me down. She went to bed with my colleagues, with the chauffeurs, with the boiler man, with the cook, even with the undertaker, only not with me. Can you imagine that?"

"Sure," said the woman doctor.

"Let me tell you," the chief physician said testily. "It was then a couple of years after graduation, and I was a big shot. I believed that every woman was attainable, and I had succeeded in proving this with relatively hard to get women. And look, I came to grief with this readily attainable girl."

"If I know you, you certainly must have a theory about it," said Dr. Havel.

"I do," replied the chief physician. "Eroticism is not only a desire for the body, but to an equal extent a desire for honor. The partner you've won, who cares about you and loves you, becomes your mirror, the measure of your importance and your merits. For my little tart this was a difficult task. When you go to bed with everyone you stop believing that such a commonplace thing as making love can still have any kind of importance. And so you seek the true erotic honor in the opposite. The only man who could provide that girl with a clear gauge of her worth was one who wanted her, but whom she herself had rejected. And because she understandably longed to verify to herself that she was the most beautiful and best of women, she went about choosing this one man, whom she would honor with her refusal, very strictly and captiously. When in the end she chose me, I understood that this was an exceptional honor, and to this day I consider this my greatest erotic success."

"It's quite marvelous the way you are able to turn water into wine," said the woman doctor.

"Does it offend you that I don't consider you my greatest success?" said the chief physician. "You must understand me. Though you are a virtuous woman, I am not, nevertheless (and you don't know how much this grieves me), your first and last, while for that tart I was. Believe me, she has never forgotten me, and to this day nostalgically remembers how she rejected me. I tell this story only to bring out the analogy to Havel's rejection of Elisabet."

In Praise of Freedom

"Good God, sir." Havel let out a groan. "I hope you're not saying that in Elisabet I'm seeking an image of my human worth!"

"Certainly not," said the woman doctor caustically. "After all, you've already explained to us that Elisabet's provocativeness strikes you as an order, and you wish to retain the illusion that it is you who are choosing the woman."

"You know, although we talk about it in those terms, Doctor, it isn't like that." Havel did a bit of thinking. "I was only trying to be witty when I said to you that Elisabet's provocativeness bothers me. To tell the truth, I've had women far more provocative than she, and their provocativeness suited me quite well, because it pleasantly speeded up the course of events."

"So why the hell don't you take Elisabet?" cried the chief physician.

"Chief, your question isn't as stupid as it seemed to me at first, because I see that as a matter of fact it's hard to answer. If I'm going to be frank, then I don't know why I don't take Elisabet. I've slept with women more hideous, more provocative, and older. From this it follows that I should necessarily sleep with her too. That's what the statisticians would say. All the cybernetic machines would draw the same conclusion. And you see, perhaps for those very reasons, I don't take her. Perhaps I want to resist necessity. To trip up causality. To throw off the dismal predictability of the world's course by means of the free will of caprice."

"But why did you pick Elisabet for this?" cried the chief physician.

"Just because it's groundless. If there had been a reason, it would have been possible to find it in advance, and it would have been possible to determine my action in advance. It's just because of this groundlessness that a tiny scrap of freedom is granted us, for which we must untiringly reach out, so that in this world of iron laws there should remain a little human disorder. My dear colleagues, long live freedom," said Havel, and sadly raised his tumbler in a toast.

Whither the Responsibility of Man Extends

At this moment a new bottle appeared in the room; it drew the attention of all the doctors present. The charming, lanky young man who was standing in the doorway with it was the ward intern, Flajsman. He put the bottle (very slowly) on the table, searched (a long time) for the corkscrew, then (slowly) pushed the corkscrew into the cork, and (quite slowly) screwed it into the cork, which he then (thoughtfully) drew out. From these parentheses Flajsman's slowness is evident; however, it testified far more to his slothful self-love than to clumsiness; with self-love the young intern would gaze peacefully into his own heart, overlooking the insignificant details of the outside world.

Dr. Havel said: "All the stuff we've been chattering about here is nonsense. It isn't I who am rejecting Elisabet, but she me. Unfortunately. Anyhow, she's crazy about Flajsman."

"About me?" Flajsman raised his head from the bottle, then with slow steps returned the corkscrew to its place, came back to the table, and poured wine into the tumblers.

"You're a fine one," said the chief physician, supporting Havel. "Everybody knows this except you. Since you appeared in our ward, it's been hard to put up with her. It's been like that for two months now."

Flajsman looked (for a long time) at the chief physician and said: "I really didn't know that." And then he added: "And anyway it doesn't interest me at all."

"And what about those gentlemanly speeches of yours? That quacking about respect for women?" Havel feigned severity. "Doesn't it interest you that you cause Elisabet pain?"

"I feel pity for women, and I could never knowingly hurt them," said Flajsman. "But what I bring about involuntarily doesn't interest me, because I'm not in a position to influence it, and so I'm not responsible for it."

Then Elisabet came into the room. She evidently considered that it would be better to forget the insult and behave as if nothing had happened; so she behaved extremely unnaturally. The chief physician pushed a chair up to the table for her and filled a tumbler: "Drink, Elisabet, and forget all the wrongs that have been done you."

"Sure." Elisabet threw him a big smile and emptied the glass.

And the chief physician turned once again to Flajsman: "If a man were responsible only for what he is aware of, blockheads would be absolved in advance from any guilt whatever. Only, my dear Flajsman, a man is obliged to know. A man is responsible for his ignorance. Ignorance is a fault. And that is why nothing absolves you from your guilt, and I declare that you are a boor in regard to women, even if you dispute it."

In Praise of Platonic Love

"I'm wondering if you've got that sublet for Miss Klara yet, you know, the one you promised her?" Havel laid into Flajsman, reminding him of his vain attempts to win the heart of a certain girl (known to all those present).

"No, I haven't, but I'm taking care of it."

"It just happens that Flajsman behaves like a gentleman toward women. Our colleague Flajsman doesn't lead women by the nose," the woman doctor said, standing up for the intern.

"I can't bear cruelty toward women, because I have pity for them," the intern repeated.

"All the same Klara hasn't given herself to you," said Elisabet to Flajsman, and she started to laugh in a very improper way, so that the chief physician was once again forced to take the floor:

"She gave herself, she didn't give herself, it isn't nearly so important as you think, Elisabet. It is well known that Abelard was castrated, but that he and Heloise nonetheless remained faithfully in love. Their love was immortal. George Sand lived for seven years with Frédéric Chopin, immaculate as a virgin, and there isn't a chance in a million that you could compete with them when it comes to love! I don't want to introduce into this sublime context the case of the girl who by rejecting me gave me the highest reward of love. But note this well, my dear Elisabet, love is connected far more loosely with what you so incessantly think about than it might seem. Surely you don't doubt that Klara loves Flajsman! She's nice to him, but nevertheless she rejects him. This sounds illogical to you, but love is precisely that which is illogical."

"What's illogical in that?" Elisabet once again laughed in an improper way. "Klara cares about the apartment. That's why she's nice to Flajsman: but she doesn't feel like sleeping with him, maybe because she's sleeping with someone else. But that guy can't get her an apartment."

At that moment Flajsman raised his head and said: "You're getting on my nerves. You're like an adolescent. What if shame restrains a woman? That wouldn't occur to you, would it? What if she has some disease she's hiding from me? A surgical scar that disfigures her? Women are capable of being terribly ashamed. But you, Elisabet, you know almost nothing about this."

"Or else," said the chief physician, coming to Flajsman's aid, "when Klara is face to face with Flajsman, she is so petrified by the anguish of love that she cannot make love with him. Elisabet, can't you imagine that you could love someone so terribly that just because of it you couldn't go to bed with him?"

Elisabet confessed that she couldn't imagine that.

The Signal

At this point we can stop following the conversation for a while (they go on uninterruptedly discussing trivia) and mention that all this time Flajsman has been trying to catch the woman doctor's eye, for he has found her terribly attractive since the time (it was about a month before) he first saw her. The sublimity of her thirty years dazzled him. Until now he'd known her only in passing, and today for the first time he had the opportunity of spending a longer time in the same room with her. It seemed to him that every now and then she returned his look, and this excited him.

After one such exchange of glances, the woman doctor got up for no reason at all, walked over to the window, and said, "It's gorgeous out. There's a full moon . . . ," and then she again reached out to Flajsman with a fleeting look.

Flajsman wasn't blind to such situations, and he at once grasped that it was a signal—a signal for him. He felt his chest swelling. His chest is a sensitive instrument, worthy of Stradivarius's workshop. From time to time he would feel the aforementioned swelling, and each time he was certain that this swelling had the inevitability of an omen announcing the advent of something great and unprecedented, something exceeding all his dreams.

This time he was partly stupefied by the swelling and partly (in the corner of his mind the stupor hadn't reached) amazed: How was it that his desire had such power that at its summons reality submissively hurried to come into being? Continuing to marvel at its power, he was on the lookout for the conversation to become more heated so that the arguers would forget about his presence. As soon as this happened, he slipped out of the room.

The Handsome Young Man
with His Arms Folded

The ward where this impromptu symposium was taking place was on the ground floor of an attractive pavilion, situated (close to other pavilions) in the large
hospital garden. Now Flajsman entered this garden. He
leaned against the tall trunk of a plane tree, lit a cigarette, and gazed at the sky. It was summer, fragrances
floated through the air, and a round moon was sus-
pended in the black sky.

He tried to imagine the course of future events: The
woman doctor who had indicated to him a little while
before that he should step outside would bide her time
until her baldpate was more involved in the conversation than in watching her, and then probably she would
inconspicuously announce that a small, intimate need
compelled her to absent herself from the company for a
moment.

And what else would happen? He deliberately didn't
want to imagine anything else. His swelling chest was
apprising him of a love affair, and that was enough for
him. He believed in his own good fortune, he believed
in his star of love, and he believed in the woman doctor. Pampered by his self-assurance (a self-assurance
that was always a bit amazed at itself), he lapsed into
agreeable passivity. That is to say he always saw himself as an attractive, successful, well-loved man, and it
gratified him to await a love affair with his arms folded,

so to speak. He believed that precisely this posture was bound to provoke both women and fate.

Perhaps at this opportunity it is worth mentioning that Flajsman very often, if not uninterruptedly (and with self-love), *saw* himself; so he was continuously accompanied by a double and this made his solitude quite amusing. This time he not only stood leaning against the plane tree smoking, but he simultaneously observed himself with self-love. He saw how he was standing (handsome and boyish) leaning against the plane tree, nonchalantly smoking. He diverted himself for some time with this sight, until finally he heard light footsteps coming in his direction from the pavilion. He purposely didn't turn around. He drew once more on his cigarette, exhaled the smoke, and looked at the sky. When the steps were quite close to him, he said in a tender, winning voice: "I knew that you would come."

Urination

"That wasn't so hard to figure out," the chief physician replied. "I always prefer to take a leak in nature rather than in modern facilities, which are foul. Here my little golden fountain will before long wondrously unite with the soil, the grass, the earth. For, Flajsman, I arose from the dust, and now at least in part I shall return to the dust. A leak in nature is a religious ceremony, by means of which we promise the earth that in the end we'll return to it entirely."

As Flajsman remained silent, the chief physician questioned him: "And what about you? Did you come to look at the moon?" And as Flajsman stubbornly continued to be silent the chief physician said: "You're a real lunatic, Flajsman. And that's why I like you so much." Flajsman perceived the chief physician's words as mockery, and wanting to keep his image, he said aloofly: "Let's leave the moon out of it. I came to take a piss too."

"My dear Flajsman," said the chief physician very gently, "from you I consider this an exceptional show of kindness toward your aging boss."

Then they both stood under the plane tree performing the act the chief physician with untiring rapture and in ever new images had described as a sacred rite.

ACT TWO

The Handsome and Sarcastic Young Man

Then they went back together down the long corridor, and the chief physician put his arm around the intern's shoulder in a brotherly fashion. The intern was certain that the jealous baldpate had detected the woman doctor's signal and was now mocking him with his friendly effusions! Of course he couldn't remove his boss's arm from his shoulder, but all the more did anger accumulate in his heart. And the only thing that consoled him was that not only was he full of anger, but also he immediately *saw* himself in this angry state, and was pleased with the furious young man who returned to the staff room and to everyone's surprise was suddenly an utterly different person: sarcastic, witty, almost demonic.

When they both actually entered the staff room, Elisabet was standing in the middle of the room, twisting about horribly from the waist and emitting some singing sounds in a low voice. Dr. Havel looked at the floor, and the woman doctor, so as to relieve the shock of the two new arrivals, explained: "Elisabet is dancing."

"She's a bit drunk," Havel added.

Elisabet didn't stop swaying her hips while gyrating the upper part of her body around the lowered head of the seated Havel.

"Wherever did you learn such a beautiful dance?" asked the chief physician.

Flajsman, bursting with sarcasm, let out a conspicuous laugh: "Ha-ha-ha! A beautiful dance! Ha-ha-ha!"

"I saw it at a striptease joint in Vienna," Elisabet replied.

"Now, now," the chief physician scolded her gently. "Since when do our nurses go to strip joints?"

"I don't suppose it's forbidden, Chief!" Elisabet gyrated the upper part of her body around the chief physician.

Bile shot up through Flajsman's body and escaped through his lips: "You should take a bromide," he said, "instead of stripping. You're going to end up raping us!"

"Don't worry. I don't cradle-snatch," Elisabet snapped back, and she gyrated the upper part of her body around Havel.

"And did you like the striptease?" The chief physician went on questioning her in a fatherly way.

"Yes, I did!" replied Elisabet. "There was a Swedish girl there with gigantic breasts, but see, mine are more beautiful" (with those words she stroked her breasts). "And also there was a girl who pretended to be bathing in soap bubbles in some sort of cardboard tub, and a half-black girl who masturbated right in front of the audience—that was best of all!"

"Ha-ha!" said Flajsman at the height of his fiendish sarcasm. "Masturbation, that's just the thing for you!"

125

Grief in the Shape of a Backside

Elisabet went on dancing, but her audience was probably far worse than the one at the Vienna strip joint: Havel lowered his head, the woman doctor watched scornfully, Flajsman negatively, and the chief physician with fatherly forbearance. And Elisabet's backside, covered with the white material of a nurse's apron, circled around the room like a beautifully round sun, but an extinct and dead sun (wrapped up in a white shroud), a sun doomed to pitiful redundance by the indifferent and distracted eyes of the doctors present.

At one moment when it seemed that Elisabet would really begin to throw off her clothing, the chief physician protested in an uneasy voice: "Come, Elisabet dear! I hope you don't want to demonstrate the Vienna show here for us!"

"What are you afraid of, Chief! At least you'd see how a naked female should really look!" screeched Elisabet, and then she turned again to Havel, threatening him with her breasts: "What is it, Havel my pet? You're acting as if you were at a funeral. Raise your head! Did someone die on you? Did someone die on you? Look at me! I'm alive, at least! I'm not dying! For the time being I'm still alive! I'm alive!" and with these words her backside was no longer a backside, but grief itself, splendidly formed grief dancing around the room.

"You should quit, Elisabet," said Havel, his eyes fixed on the floor.

"Quit?" said Elisabet. "But it's you I'm dancing for! And now I'll perform a striptease for you! A great striptease!" and she undid her smock, and with a dancing movement cast it onto the desk.

The chief physician once again protested timidly: "Elisabet, my dear, it would be beautiful if you performed your striptease for us, but somewhere else. You must realize that this is a hospital."

The Great Striptease

"Chief, I know what I'm allowed to do!" replied Elisabet. She was now in her pale-blue state uniform with the white collar, and she didn't stop wiggling.

Then she put her hands on her hips and slid them up both sides of her body and all the way up above her head. Then she ran her right hand along her raised left arm and then her left hand along her right arm, then with both arms made a gesture in Flajsman's direction as if she were tossing him her blouse. It startled Flajsman, and he jumped. "Mama's boy, you dropped it!" she yelled at him.

Then she put her hands on her hips again and this time slid them down both legs. When she had bent over, she raised first her right and then her left leg. Then, staring at the chief physician, she flung out her right arm, tossing him an imaginary skirt. At the same time the chief physician extended his hand with the fingers spread out, and immediately clasped them into a fist. Then he put this hand on his knee and with the fingers of the other hand blew Elisabet a kiss.

After some more wriggling and dancing, Elisabet rose on tiptoe, bent her arms at the elbows, and put them behind her back. Then with dancing movements, she brought her arms forward, stroked her left shoulder with her right palm and her right shoulder with her left palm and again made a gliding movement with her arm, this time in Havel's direction. He also distractedly moved his arm a little.

Now Elisabet straightened up and began to stride majestically around the room; she went around to all four spectators in turn, thrusting at each of them the symbolic nakedness of the upper part of her body. Eventually she stopped in front of Havel, once again began wiggling her hips, and bending down slightly, slid both her arms down her sides and again (as before) raised first one, then the other leg. After that she triumphantly stood up straight, raising her right hand as if she were holding an invisible slip between her thumb and index finger. With this hand she again waved with a gliding movement in Havel's direction.

Then she stood on tiptoe again, posing in the full glory of her fictional nakedness. She was no longer looking at anyone, not even at Havel, but with the half-closed eyes of her half-turned head she was staring down at her own twisting body.

Suddenly her showy posture relaxed, and Elisabet sat down on Dr. Havel's knee. "I'm bushed," she said, yawning. She stretched out her hand for Havel's glass and took a drink. "Doctor," she said to Havel, "you don't have some kind of pep pill, do you? I don't want to go to sleep!"

"Anything for you, dear Elisabet!" said Havel. He lifted Elisabet off his knees, set her on a chair, and went over to the dispensary. There he found some strong sleeping pills and gave two of them to Elisabet.

"Will this pick me up?" she asked.

"Or my name isn't Havel," said Havel.

Elisabet's Words at Parting

When Elisabet had swallowed both pills, she wanted to sit on Havel's knee again, but Havel moved his legs aside so that she fell to the floor.

Havel immediately felt sorry about this, because in fact he hadn't intended to let Elisabet fall in this ignominious way, and if he moved his legs aside, it was an unconscious movement caused by his simple aversion to touching Elisabet's backside with his legs.

So he tried now to lift her up again, but Elisabet in pitiful defiance was clinging to the floor with her whole weight.

At this moment Flajsman stood up in front of her and said: "You're drunk, you should go to bed."

Elisabet looked up from the floor with boundless scorn and (relishing the masochistic pathos of her being on the floor) said to him: "You beast. You idiot." And once again: "You idiot."

Havel once more attempted to lift her up, but she broke away from him furiously and began to sob. No one knew what to say, so her sobbing echoed through the silent room like a violin solo. Only a bit later did it occur to the woman doctor to start whistling quietly. Elisabet got up brusquely, went to the door, and as she took hold of the door handle, half-turned toward the room and said: "You beasts. You beasts. If you only knew. You don't know anything. You don't know anything."

The Chief Physician's Indictment of Flajsman

After her departure there was silence that the chief physician was the first to break. "You see, Flajsman, my boy. You say you feel sorry for women. But if you are sorry for them, why aren't you sorry for Elisabet?"

"Why should I care about her?" Flajsman protested.

"Don't pretend that you don't know anything! We told you about it a little while ago. She's crazy about you."

"Can I help it?" asked Flajsman.

"You can't," said the chief physician. "But you can help being rude to her and tormenting her. The whole evening it mattered a great deal to her what you would do, if you would look at her and smile, if you would say something nice to her. And remember what you did say to her!"

"I didn't say anything so terrible to her," protested Flajsman, but his voice sounded uncertain.

"Nothing so terrible, eh?" the chief physician said with irony. "You made fun of her dance, even though she was dancing only for your sake, you recommended a bromide for her, you claimed there was nothing for her but masturbation. Nothing terrible? When she was doing her striptease you let her blouse fall on the floor."

"What blouse?" protested Flajsman.

"Her blouse," said the physician. "And don't play the fool. In the end you sent her off to bed although a moment before she had taken a pep pill."

"But it was Havel she was running after, not me!" Flajsman continued to protest.

"Don't put on an act," said the chief physician sternly. "What could she do if you weren't paying attention to her? She was trying to provoke you. And she was only longing for a few crumbs of jealousy from you. Talk about a gentleman!"

"Don't torment him anymore," said the woman doctor. "He's cruel, but he's young."

"He's the avenging archangel," said Havel.

Mythological Roles

"Yes, indeed," said the woman doctor, "look at him: a wicked, handsome archangel."

"We are a real mythological group," the chief physician sleepily observed, "because you are Diana. Cold, athletic, and spiteful."

"And you are a satyr. Grown old, lecherous, and garrulous," said the woman doctor. "And Havel is Don Juan. He's not old, but he's getting old."

"Not at all! Havel is death," the chief physician objected, returning to his old thesis.

The End of the Don Juans

"If you ask me whether I'm Don Juan or death, I must incline, though unhappily, toward the chief physician's opinion," said Havel, taking a long drink. "Don Juan, after all, was a conqueror. And in capital letters. A Great Conqueror. But I ask you, how can you be a conqueror in a domain where no one refuses you, where everything is possible and everything is permitted? Don Juan's era has come to an end. Today Don Juan's descendant no longer *conquers*, he only *collects*. The figure of the Great Collector has taken the place of the Great Conqueror, only the collector has nothing in common with Don Juan. Don Juan was a tragic figure. He was burdened by his guilt. He sinned gaily and laughed at God. He was a blasphemer and ended up in hell.

"Don Juan bore on his shoulders a dramatic burden that the Great Collector has no idea of, because in his world every burden has lost its weight. Boulders have become feathers. In the conqueror's world, a single glance was as important as ten years of the most ardent love-making in the collector's realm.

"Don Juan was a master, while the collector is a slave. Don Juan arrogantly transgressed conventions and laws. The Great Collector only obediently, by the sweat of his brow, complies with conventions and the law, because collecting has become good manners, good form, and almost an obligation. After all, if I'm burdened by any guilt, then it's only because I don't take on Elisabet.

"The Great Collector knows nothing of tragedy or drama. Eroticism, which used to be the greatest instigator of catastrophes, has become, thanks to him, like breakfasts and dinners, like stamp collecting and table tennis, if not like a ride on the streetcar or shopping. He has brought it into the ordinary round of events. He has turned it into a stage on which real drama never takes place. Alas, my friends," rants Havel, "my loves (if I may call them that) are a stage on which nothing is happening.

"My dear doctor and you, dear Chief. You've put Don Juan and death in opposition to each other. By sheer chance and inadvertence, you've grasped the essence of the matter. Look. Don Juan struggled against the impossible. And that is a very human thing to do. But in the realm of the Great Collector, nothing's impossible, because it is the realm of death. The Great Collector is death looking for tragedy, drama, and love. Death, which came looking for Don Juan. In hellfire, where the Commander sent him, Don Juan is alive. But in the world of the Great Collector, where passions and feelings flutter through space like feathers—in this world he is forever dead.

"Not at all, my dear Doctor," said Havel sadly, "Don Juan and I, not at all! What would I have given to have seen the Commander and to have felt in my soul the terrible burden of his curse and to have felt the greatness of the tragedy growing within me! Not at all, Doctor, I am at most a figure of comedy, and I do not owe even that to my own efforts, but to Don Juan, because only against the historical background of his tragic gaiety can you to some extent perceive the comic sadness of my womaniz-

ing existence, which without this gauge would be nothing but gray banality in a tedious setting."

Further Signals

Havel, fatigued by his long speech (in the course of it the
sleepy chief physician had almost nodded off twice), fell
silent. Only after an appropriate instant full of emotion
did the woman doctor break the silence: "I hadn't suspected, Doctor, that you could speak so fluently. You've
portrayed yourself as a figure of comedy, gray, dull, a zero
in fact. Unfortunately the way you spoke was somewhat
too sublime. You're so damned cunning: calling yourself
a beggar, but choosing words so majestic that you sound
more like a king. You're an old fraud, Havel. Vain even as
you vilify yourself. You're simply an old fraud."

Flajsman laughed loudly, for he believed to his great
satisfaction that in the woman doctor's words he could
detect scorn for Havel. So, encouraged by her mockery
and his own laughter, he went over to the window and
said meaningfully: "What a night!"

"Yes," said the woman doctor, "a gorgeous night.
And Havel is playing death! Have you noticed, Havel,
what a beautiful night it is?"

"Of course he hasn't," said Flajsman. "For Havel

one woman is like another, one night like another, winter like summer. Doctor Havel refuses to distinguish the secondary characteristics of things."

"You've seen right through me," said Havel.

Flajsman concluded that this time his rendezvous with the woman doctor would be successful. The chief physician had drunk a great deal and the sleepiness that had overcome him in the last few minutes had considerably blunted his wariness. That being so, Flajsman inconspicuously remarked: "Oh, this bladder of mine!" and, throwing a glance in the woman doctor's direction, he went out the door.

Gas

Walking along the corridor, he recalled that throughout the evening the woman doctor had been ironically making fun of both men, the chief physician and Havel, whom she just now had very aptly called frauds. He was astonished that it was happening once again; he marveled anew each time it happened, because it happened so regularly: Women liked him, they preferred him to experienced men. In the case of the woman doctor, this was a great, new, and unexpected triumph, since she was obviously choosy, intelligent, and a bit (but pleasantly) haughty.

It was with these pleasant thoughts that Flajsman walked down the long corridor to the exit. When he was almost at the swinging doors leading to the garden, he suddenly smelled the odor of gas. He stopped and sniffed. The smell was concentrated at the door leading to the nurses' small staff room. All at once Flajsman realized that he was terribly frightened.

First he wanted to run back quickly and bring Havel and the chief physician, but then he decided to take hold of the door handle (perhaps because he assumed that it would be locked, if not barricaded). But surprisingly enough the door was open. In the room a strong ceiling light was on, illuminating a large, naked, female body lying on the couch. Flajsman looked around the room and hurried over to the small range. He turned off the gas jet. Then he ran to the window and flung it wide open.

A Remark in Parentheses

(One can say that Flajsman had acted promptly and with great presence of mind. There was one thing, however, that he wasn't able to record with a sufficiently cool head. It is true that for an instant he stood gaping at Elisabet's naked body, but shock had overcome him to such a degree that beneath its veil he did not realize what we from an advantageous distance can fully appreciate:

Elisabet's body was magnificent. She was lying on her back with her head turned slightly to the side and one shoulder slightly bent inward toward the other, so that her beautiful breasts pressed against each other and showed their full shape. One of her legs was stretched out and the other was slightly bent at the knee, so that it was possible to see the remarkable fullness of her thighs and the exceptionally dense black of her bush.)

The Call for Help

Having opened the door and window wide, Flajsman ran out into the corridor and began to call for help. Everything that followed then took place in a brisk and matter-of-fact way: artificial respiration, phoning the emergency room, a gurney for moving the sick woman to the doctor on duty, more artificial respiration, resuscitation, a blood transfusion, and finally a deep sign of relief when it was clear that Elisabet's life had been saved.

ACT THREE
Who Said What

When all four doctors left the emergency room for the courtyard, they looked exhausted.

The chief physician said: "Poor Elisabet spoiled our symposium."

The woman doctor said: "Unsatisfied women always bring bad luck."

Havel said: "It's odd. She had to turn on the gas for us to notice that she has a beautiful body."

At these words Flajsman gave Havel a (long) look and said: "I'm no longer in the mood for drinking or trying to be witty. Good night." And he headed toward the hospital exit.

Flajsman's Theory

His colleagues' words disgusted Flajsman. In them he saw the callousness of aging men and women, the cruelty of their mature years, which rose before his youth like a hostile barrier. For this reason he was glad to be alone, and he purposely went on foot, because he wanted fully to experience and enjoy his agitation. With pleasurable terror he kept repeating that Elisabet had been within moments of death, and that he would have been responsible for this death.

Of course he knew well that suicide does not have a single cause but, for the most part, a constellation of causes, yet on the other hand he couldn't deny that the one, and probably the decisive cause was he himself through the simple fact of his existence and of his behavior that night.

Now he emphatically blamed himself. He called himself an egotist, who out of vanity had been engrossed in his own erotic successes. He derided himself for allowing himself to be dazzled by the woman doctor's interest. He blamed himself for turning Elisabet into a mere object, a vessel into which he had poured his rage when the jealous chief physician had thwarted his nocturnal rendezvous. By what right had he behaved like this toward an innocent human being?

The young intern, however, was not a primitive creature; every one of his states of mind encompassed a dialectic of assertion and negation, so that now his inner counsel for the defense was rebutting his inner prosecutor: The sarcastic remarks that he had made about Elisabet had been uncalled for, but they would hardly have had such tragic results if it hadn't been for the fact that Elisabet loved him. However, was Flajsman to blame because someone had fallen in love with him? Did he as a result become automatically become responsible for this woman?

At this question he paused for a moment. It seemed to him to be the key to the whole mystery of human exis-

tence. He stopped walking and with complete seriousness answered himself: Yes, he had been wrong when he
had tried to persuade the chief physician that he was not
responsible for what he involuntarily caused. Wasn't it
actually possible to reduce himself only to the part of
him that was conscious and intentional? Didn't what he
had involuntarily caused also belong to the sphere of his
personality? Who else but he could be responsible for
that? Yes, he was guilty; guilty of Elisabet's love; guilty
of not knowing about it; guilty of paying no attention;
guilty. He had come close to killing a human being.

The Chief Physician's Theory

While Flajsman was absorbed in his self-searching
deliberations, the chief physician, Havel, and the woman doctor returned to the staff room. They really no
longer felt like drinking. For a while they remained
silent, and then Havel sighed: "I wonder what put that
crazy idea into Elisabet's head."

"No sentimentality, please, Doctor," said the chief
physician. "When a person does something so asinine,
I refuse to be moved. Besides, if you hadn't been so
obstinate and had done long ago with her what you
don't hesitate to do with everyone else, it wouldn't have
come to this."

"Thank you for making me responsible for a suicide," said Havel.

"Let's be precise," replied the chief physician. "It wasn't a question of suicide but of a demonstration of suicide set up in such a way that a disaster would not occur. My dear Doctor, when someone wants to be asphyxiated by gas, he begins by locking the door. And not only that, he seals up the crevices so that the gas won't be located until as late as possible. Elisabet was not thinking about death, she was thinking about you.

"God knows how many weeks she's been looking forward to being on night duty with you, and since the beginning of the evening she's been brazenly making advances toward you. But you were hardhearted. And the more hardhearted you were, the more she drank and the more blatant she became. She talked nonsense, danced, wanted to do a striptease.

"You see, I wonder if after all there's something touching in all this. When she could attract neither your eyes nor your ears she staked everything on your sense of smell and turned on the gas. Before turning it on, she undressed. She knows that she has a beautiful body, and she wanted to force you to discover this. Remember how when she was standing in the doorway she said: *If you only knew. You don't know anything. You don't know anything.* So now you do know: Elisabet has an ugly face but a beautiful body. You yourself admitted it. You see, she didn't reason so altogether stupidly. I wonder if you'll now finally be prevailed on."

"Maybe." Havel shrugged his shoulders.

"Certainly," said the chief physician.

Havel's Theory

"What you say, Chief, has some plausibility, but there's an error in your reasoning: You overestimate my role in this drama. Because it's not about me. It wasn't only I who refused to go to bed with Elisabet. Nobody wanted to go to bed with Elisabet.

"When you asked me earlier why I didn't want to go to bed with Elisabet, I told you some rubbish about the beauty of caprice and how I wanted to retain my freedom. But those were only stupid witticisms with which I obscured the truth. For the truth is just the reverse and not at all flattering: I refused Elisabet just because I'm incapable of behaving like a free man. Not to sleep with Elisabet is the fashion. No one sleeps with her, and even if someone did sleep with her, he would never admit it because everyone would laugh at him. Fashion is a terrible martinet, and I've slavishly submitted to it. At the same time, Elisabet is a mature woman and this has dulled her wits. And maybe it's *my* refusal that's dulled her wits the most, because, it's well known that I go to bed with everyone. But the fashion was dearer to me that Elisabet's wits.

"And you're right, Chief, she knows that she has a beautiful body, and so she considered her situation sheer absurdity and injustice and was protesting against it. Remember how she never stopped attracing attention to her body all evening. When she talked about the Swedish stripper she saw in Vienna, she stroked her breasts and declared they were more beautiful than the Swede's. Remember how her breasts and her backside filled the room this evening like a mob of demonstrators. Actually, Chief, it really was a demonstration.

"And remember that striptease of hers, just remember how deeply she was experiencing it! It was the saddest striptease I've ever seen. She was passionately trying to strip and at the same time she still remained in the hated confinement of her nurse's uniform. She was trying to strip and couldn't. And although she knew that she wouldn't strip, she was trying to, because she wanted to communicate to us her sad and unrealizable desire to strip. Chief, she wasn't stripping, she was singing the elegy of stripping, singing about the impossibility of stripping, about the impossibility of making love, about the impossibility of living! And we didn't even want to hear it. We looked at the floor and we were unsympathetic."

"You romantic womanizer! Do you really believe that she wanted to die?" the chief physician shouted at Havel.

"Remember," said Havel, "how while she was dancing, she kept saying to me: *I'm still alive! For the time being I'm still alive!* Do you remember? From the moment she began to dance, she knew what she was going to do."

"And why did she want to die naked, eh? What kind of an explanation do you have for that?"

"She wanted to step into the arms of death as one steps into the arms of a lover. That's why she undressed, did her hair, and put on makeup—"

"And that's why she left the door unlocked, what about that? Please don't try to persuade yourself that she really wanted to die!"

"Maybe she didn't know exactly what she wanted. After all, do you know what you want? Which of us knows that? She wanted to die and she didn't. She quite sincerely wanted to die, and at the same time (equally sincerely) she wanted to prolong the act that was leading her to death and making her feel increased in stature. Of course, she didn't want us to see her after she had turned dark and become bad smelling and disfigured by death. She wanted us to see her beautiful, underestimated body that in all its glory was going to copulate with death. She wanted us, at least at so vital a moment as this, to envy death this body and long for it."

The Woman Doctor's Theory

"My dear gentlemen," protested the woman doctor, who had been silently listening attentively to both doctors, "so far as I, as a woman, can judge, you've both spoken logically. Your theories are plausible in themselves and astonishing, because they reveal such a deep knowledge of life. They contain only one little imperfection: there isn't an iota of truth in them. Elisabet didn't want to commit suicide. Not genuine suicide, nor staged. Neither."

For a moment the woman doctor relished the effect of her words, then she went on. "My dear gentlemen, I detect a bad conscience in you. When we were coming back from the emergency room, you avoided the nurses' small staff room. You no longer even wanted to see it. But I took a good look around while they were giving Elisabet artificial respiration. A small pot was on the range. Elisabet was making herself some coffee and she fell asleep. The water boiled over and put out the flames."

Both the male doctors hurried with the woman doctor to the nurses' staff room, and there was indeed a pot on the burner with a bit of water still in it.

"But in that case, why was she naked?" said the astonished chief physician.

"Look." The woman doctor pointed to the corners of the room: on the floor beneath the window lay a pale blue uniform, up on the white medicine chest hung a bra, and in the opposite corner on the floor was a pair of white underpants. "Elisabet threw her clothes in different directions, bearing witness to the fact that she wanted at least to complete the striptease, even if only for herself alone. The striptease you, cautious Chief, had blocked!

"When she was naked, she probably felt tired. This didn't suit her, because she hadn't given up her hopes for the night. She knew that we were all going to leave and that Havel would remain here alone. That's surely why she asked for pep pills. She decided to make some coffee for herself and put the pot on the burner. Then once again she caught sight of her body and this aroused her. My dear gentlemen, Elisabet had one advantage over all of you. She couldn't see her head. So to herself she was flawlessly beautiful. She was aroused by this, and she lasciviously lay down on the couch. But sleep obviously overwhelmed her before sensual delight did."

"Of course," Havel said. "Especially since I gave her sleeping pills!"

"That's just like you," said the woman doctor. "So is anything still unclear to you?"

"There is," said Havel. "Remember those things she said: *I'm not dying! I'm alive. For the time being I'm still alive!* And those last words of hers: she said them so pathetically, as if they were words of farewell: *If you only knew. You don't know anything. You don't know anything.*"

"But Havel," said the woman doctor, "as if you didn't

know that ninety-nine percent of all statements are idle talk. Don't you yourself talk mostly just for the sake of talking?"

The doctors kept talking for a little while longer and then all three went out in front of the pavilion. The chief physician and the woman doctor shook hands with Havel and walked away.

Through the Summer Night Floated the Fragrance of Flowers

Flajsman finally arrived at the suburban street where he lived with his parents in a small villa surrounded by a garden. He opened the gate and sat down on a bench, above which twined the roses carefully tended by his mother.

Through the summer night floated the fragrance of flowers, and the words "guilty," "egotism," "beloved," "death" rose in Flajsman's chest and filled him with uplifting delight, so that he had the impression that he had wings on his back.

In the first flush of melancholy happiness he realized that he was loved as never before. Certainly several women had expressed their affection for him, but now he had to be soberly truthful with himself: Had it always been love? Hadn't he sometimes been subject to illusions? Hadn't he sometimes talked himself into things? Wasn't Klara perhaps actually more calculating than enamored? Didn't the apartment he was getting for her matter more to her than he himself? In the light of Elisabet's act, everything paled.

Through the air floated only important words, and Flajsman said to himself that love has but one measure, and that is death. At the end of true love is death, and only the love that ends in death is love.

Through the night the fragrance floated, and Flajsman wondered: Would anyone ever love him as much as this ugly woman does? But what is beauty or ugliness compared with love? What is the ugliness of a face compared with an emotion in whose greatness the absolute itself is mirrored?

(The absolute? Yes. This was a young man only recently cast out into the adult world, which is full of uncertainties. However much he ran after girls, above all he was seeking a comforting, boundless, redeeming embrace, which would save him from the horrifying relativity of the freshly discovered world.)

ACT FOUR
The Woman Doctor's Return

Dr. Havel had been lying on the couch for a while, covered with a light woolen blanket, when he heard a tapping on the window. In the moonlight he caught sight of the woman doctor's face. He opened the window and asked: "What's the matter?"

"Let me in!" said the woman doctor, and she hurried toward the building entrance.

Havel buttoned his shirt, heaved a sigh, and left the room.

When he unlocked the pavilion door, the woman doctor without so much as an explanation rushed into the staff room, and only when she had seated herself in an armchair opposite Havel did she begin to explain that she hadn't been able to go home; only now, she said, did she realize how upset she was. She would be unable to sleep, and she asked Havel to talk to her for a bit, so she could calm down.

Havel didn't believe a word of what the woman doctor was telling him, and he was ungentlemanly enough (or careless) to let her see this.

That is why the woman doctor said: "Of course you don't believe me, because you're convinced that I've only come to sleep with you."

The doctor made a gesture of denial, but the woman doctor continued: "You're a conceited Don Juan! Naturally, all the women who set eyes on you think of nothing but that. And you, bored and disgusted, carry out your sad mission."

Once again Havel made a gesture of denial, but the woman doctor, having lit a cigarette and nonchalantly exhaled smoke, continued: "My poor Don Juan, don't worry. I haven't come to bother you. You're not at all like death. That is just our dear chief physician's little joke. You don't take everything, because not every woman would allow you to take her. I guarantee that I, for example, am absolutely immune to you."

"Did you come to tell me that?"

"Perhaps. I came to comfort you, by telling you that you are not like death. That I wouldn't let myself be taken."

Havel's Morality

"It's nice of you," said Havel. "It's nice that you wouldn't let yourself be taken and that you came to tell me that. I'm really not like death. Not only won't I take Elisabet, but I wouldn't even take you."

"Oh!" said the woman doctor.

"By this I don't mean that I'm not attracted to you. On the contrary."

"That's better," said the woman doctor.

"Yes, you do attract me very much."

"So why wouldn't you take me? Because I don't care about you?"

"No, I don't think it has anything to do with that," said Havel.

"Then with what?"

"You're the chief physician's mistress."

"So?"

"The chief physician is jealous. It would hurt him."

"Do you have moral inhibitions?" said the woman doctor with a laugh.

"You know," said Havel, "in my life I've had enough affairs with women to teach me to respect friendship between men. Such friendship unblemished by the idiocy of eroticism is the only value I've found in life."

"Do you consider the chief physician a friend?"

"He's done a lot for me."

"More, no doubt, for me," replied the woman doctor.

"Maybe," said Havel, "but it isn't a question of gratitude. He's a friend, that's all. He's a great guy. And he really cares about you. If I did happen to make a play for you, I would have to consider myself a real bastard."

Slander of the Chief Physician

"I never expected," said the woman doctor, "that I would hear such heartfelt odes to friendship from you! You present me, Doctor, with a new, unexpected image of yourself. Not only do you, contrary to all expectations, have a capacity for emotion, but you bestow it (and this is touching) on an old, bald, gray-haired gentleman, who is noteworthy only because of how funny he is. Did you notice him this evening? How he continuously shows off? He's always trying to prove things no one can believe.

"First, he wants to prove that he's witty. Did you notice? He incessantly talked nonsense; he entertained the company; he made cracks about Doctor Havel being like death; he concocted paradoxes about the misfortune of a happy marriage (as if I wasn't hearing it for the fiftieth time!); he took pains to lead Flajsman by the nose (as if it required any brilliance to do that!).

"Second, he tries to show that he's a friendly man. In reality, of course, he doesn't like anybody with hair on his head, but because of this he tries all the harder. He flattered you, he flattered me, he was kind to Elisabet in a fatherly way, and he even kidded Flajsman so cautiously that he wouldn't notice it.

"And third, and this is the main thing, he tries to prove that he's an ace. He tries desperately to hide his present appearance beneath his former appearance.

Unfortunately it no longer exists, and not one of us remembers it. Surely you noticed how neatly he introduced the incident about the tart who refused him, only so as to evoke his youthful, irresistible face and make us forget his pitiful bald head."

A Defense of the Chief Physician

"Everything you say is pretty much true, Doctor," replied Havel. "But that provides even more reasons for me to like the chief physician, because all this is closer to me than you suspect. Why should I mock a bald spot that I won't escape? Why should I mock those earnest efforts of the chief physician not to be who he is?

"An old man will either make the best of the fact that he is what he is, a lamentable wreck of his former self, or he won't. But what should he do if he doesn't make the best of it? There remains nothing but to pretend not to be what he is. There remains nothing but to recreate, by means of a difficult pretense, everything that he no longer is, that has been lost: to invent, act, and mime his gaiety, vitality, and friendliness; to evoke his youthful self and to try to merge with it and have it replace what he has become. In the chief physician's game of pretense I see myself, my own future—

if, of course, I have enough strength to defy resignation, which is certainly a worse evil than this sad pretense.

"Maybe you've diagnosed the chief physician correctly. But I like him even better for it and I could never
hurt him, so it follows that I could never do anything
with you."

The Woman Doctor's Reply

"My dear Doctor," replied the woman doctor, "there
are fewer differences between us than you suppose. I
like him too. I'm also sorry for him—just like you. And
I have more to be grateful for from him than you. Without him I wouldn't have such a good position. (Anyhow, you know this, everybody knows this only too
well.) Do you think that I lead him by the nose? That I
cheat on him? That I have other lovers? With what relish they'd inform him about that! I don't want to hurt
him or myself, and that's why I'm more tied down than
you can imagine. But I'm glad that we two understand
each other now. Because you are the one man with
whom I can afford to be unfaithful to the chief physician. You really do like him and you would never hurt
him. You will be scrupulously discreet. I can depend on

you. I can go to bed with you—" and she sat down on
Havel's knee and began to unbutton his clothes.

What Did Dr. Havel Do?

Guess . . .

ACT FIVE
In a Vortex of Noble Sentiments

After the night came morning, and Flajsman went into the back garden to cut some roses. Then he took the streetcar to the hospital.

Elisabet was in a private room in the emergency ward. Flajsman took a seat near her bed, put the flowers on the night table, and her hand to take her pulse.

"Well now, are you feeling better?" he asked.

"Yes," said Elisabet.

And Flajsman said warmly: "You shouldn't have done such a silly thing, my girl."

"You're right," said Elisabet, "but I fell asleep. I put on the coffee water, and I fell asleep like an idiot."

Flajsman sat gaping at Elisabet, because he hadn't expected such nobility: Elisabet didn't want to burden him with remorse, she didn't want to burden him with her love, and therefore she was renouncing it!

He stroked her face, and carried away by emotion, addressed her tenderly: "I know everything. You don't need to lie. But I do thank you for that lie."

He understood that he wouldn't find such refinement, devotion, and consideration in any other woman, and a terrible desire to give in to this fit of rashness and ask her to become his wife swept over him. At the last moment, however, he regained his self-control (there's always enough time for a marriage proposal), and he said only this: "Elisabet, Elisabet, my girl. I brought these roses for you."

Elisabet gaped at Flajsman and said: "For me?"

"Yes, for you. Because I'm happy to be here with you. Because I'm happy that you exist at all, Elisabet. Perhaps I love you. Perhaps I love you very much. But probably just for this reason it would be better if we remain as we are. I think a man and a woman love each other all the more when they don't live together and when they know about each other only that they exist, and when they are grateful to each other for the fact that they exist and that they know they exist. And that alone is enough for their happiness. I thank you, dear Elisabet, I thank you for existing."

Elisabet didn't understand any of it, but a foolish, blissful smile full of vague happiness and indistinct hope spread across her face.

Then Flajsman got up, squeezed Elisabet's shoulder (as a sign of discreet, self-restrained love), turned around, and left.

The Uncertainty of All Things

"Our beautiful female colleague, who looks absolutely radiant with youth today, has perhaps actually offered the most correct interpretation of the events," said the chief physician to the woman doctor and to Havel, when all three of them met in the ward. "Elisabet was making some coffee and fell asleep. At least that's what she claims."

"You see," said the woman doctor.

"I don't see anything," objected the chief physician. "As a matter of fact no one knows anything about how it really was. The pot could have been on the range already. If Elisabet wanted to turn the gas on herself, why would she take off the pot?"

"But she herself explains it that way!" argued the woman doctor.

"After she performed for us and scared us, don't be surprised that she put the blame on a pot. Don't forget that in this country would-be suicides are sent to an asylum for treatment. No one wants to go there."

"Do you like suicide stories, Chief?" asked the woman doctor.

"For once I'd like Havel to be tortured by remorse," the chief physician said, laughing.

Havel's Repentance

Havel's bad conscience heard in the chief physician's insignificant words a reproach in code, by means of which the heavens were discreetly admonishing him, and he said: "The chief physician is right. This wasn't necessarily a suicide attempt, but it could have been.

Besides, if I am to speak frankly, I wouldn't hold it against Elisabet. Tell me, where in life is there a value that would make us consider suicide uncalled for on principle! Love? Or friendship? I guarantee you that friendship is not a bit less fickle than love, and it is impossible to build anything on it. Self-love? I wish it were possible," Havel now said almost ardently, and it sounded like repentance. "But, Chief, I swear to you that I don't like myself at all."

"My dear gentlemen," said the woman doctor smiling, "if it will make the world more beautiful for you and will save your souls, please let's agree that Elisabet really did want to commit suicide. Agreed?"

A Happy Ending

"Nonsense," said the chief physician. "Quit it. Havel, don't pollute the beautiful morning air with your speeches! I'm fifteen years older than you. I am an unhappy man because I have a happy marriage, and consequently I cannot divorce. And I have an unhappy love, because the woman I love is unfortunately this doctor here! Yet all the same I like being alive!"

"That's right, that's right," said the woman doctor to the chief physician with unusual tenderness, seizing him by the hand. "I too like being alive!"

At this moment, Flajsman came up to the trio of doctors and said: "I've been to see Elisabet. She's an astonishingly honorable woman. She denied everything. She's taken it all on herself."

"You see," said the chief physician, laughing. "And Havel here was pushing us all to suicide."

"Of course," said the woman doctor. She went over to the window. "It will be a beautiful day again. The sky is so blue. What do you say about that, my dear Flajsman?"

Only a moment before Flajsman had been almost reproaching himself for having acted cunningly when he had settled everything with a bunch of roses and some nice words, but now he was glad that he hadn't rushed into anything. He heard the woman doctor's signal, and he understood it perfectly. The thread of the romance was being resumed where it had been broken off yesterday, when the odor of gas had thwarted his rendezvous with the woman doctor. He couldn't help smiling at the woman doctor even in front of the jealous chief physician.

So the story picks up from where it finished yesterday, but it seems to Flajsman that he is reentering it a far older and far stronger man. He has known a love as great as death. His chest swells, and it is the most beautiful and powerful swelling he has ever experienced. For what is inflating him so pleasurably is death: the death that has been given him as a present; splendid and comforting death.

Let the Old Dead Make Room for the Young Dead

1

He was returning home along the street of a small Bohemian town, where he had been living for several years, reconciled to his not-too-exciting life, his backbiting neighbors, and the monotonous rowdiness that surrounded him at work, and he was walking so totally without seeing (as one walks along a path traversed a hundred times) that he almost passed her by. But she had already recognized him from a distance, and coming toward him she gave him that gentle smile of hers; only at the last moment, when they had almost passed each other, did the smile ring a bell in his memory and snap him out of his drowsy state.

"I wouldn't have recognized you!" he apologized, but it was a awkward apology, because it brought them precipitously to a painful subject, about which it would have been advisable to keep silent; they had not seen each other for fifteen years and during this time they had both aged. "Have I changed so much?" she asked, and he replied that she hadn't, and even if this was a lie it wasn't an out-and-out lie, because that gentle smile (expressing demurely and restrainedly a capacity for some sort of eternal enthusiasm) emerged from the distance of many years quite unchanged, and it confused him: it evoked for him so distinctly the former appearance of this woman that he had to make a definite effort to disregard it and to see her as she was now: she was almost an old woman.

He asked her where she was going and what was on her schedule, and she replied that she had nothing else to do but wait for the train that would take her back to Prague that evening. He evinced pleasure at their unexpected meeting, and because they agreed (with good reason) that the two local cafés were overcrowded and dirty, he invited her to his bachelor apartment, which wasn't very far away; he had both coffee and tea there, and, more important, it was clean and peaceful.

2

Right from the start it had been a bad day. Her husband (twenty-five years ago she had lived here with him for a short time as a new bride, then they had moved to Prague, where he'd died ten years back) was buried, thanks to an eccentric wish in his last will and testament, in the local cemetery. At that time she had paid in advance for a ten-year lease on the grave, but a few days before, she had become afraid that the time limit had expired and that she had forgotten to renew the lease. Her first impulse had been to write the cemetery administration, but then she had realized how futile it was to correspond with the authorities, and she had come out here.

She knew the path to her husband's grave from memory, and yet today she felt all as if she was in this cemetery for the first time. She couldn't find the grave, and it seemed to her that she had gone astray. It took her a while to understand. There, where the gray sandstone monument with the name of her husband in gold lettering used to be, precisely on that spot (she confidently recognized the two neighboring graves) now stood a black marble headstone with a quite different name in gilt.

Upset, she went to the cemetery administration. There they told her that upon expiration of the leases, the graves were canceled. She reproached them for not have advised her that she should renew the lease, and they replied that there was little room in the cemetery and that *the old dead must make room for the young dead.* This exasperated her, and she told them, holding back her tears, that they knew absolutely nothing of human dignity or respect for others, but she understood that the conversation was useless. Just as she could not have prevented her husband's death, so also she was defenseless against his second death, this death of an *old dead* who is now forbidden to exist even as dead.

She went off into town, and anxiety quickly began to mingle with her sorrow as she tried to imagine how she would explain to her son the disappearance of his father's grave and how she would justify her neglect. At last fatigue overtook her: she didn't know how to pass the long hours until time for the departure of her train, for she no longer knew anyone here, and nothing encouraged her to take even a sentimental stroll, because over the years the town had changed too much, and the once familiar places looked quite strange to her now. That is why she gratefully accepted the invitation of the (half-forgotten) old acquaintance she'd met by chance: She could wash her hands in his bathroom and then sit in his soft armchair (her legs ached), look around his room, and listen to the boiling water bubbling away behind the screen that separated the kitchen nook from the room.

3

Not long ago he had turned thirty-five, and exactly at that time he had noticed that the hair on top of his head was thinning very visibly. The bald spot wasn't there yet, but its appearance was quite conceivable (the scalp was showing beneath the hair) and, more important, it was certain to appear and in the not-too-distant future. Certainly it was ridiculous to make thinning hair a matter of life or death, but he realized that baldness would change his face and that his hitherto youthful appearance (undeniably his best) was on its way out.

And now these considerations made him think about how the balance sheet of this person (with hair), who was going away bit by bit, actually stood, what he had actually experienced and enjoyed. What astounded him was the knowledge that he had experienced rather little; when he thought about this he felt embarrassed; yes, he was ashamed, because to live here on earth so long and to experience so little was ignominious.

What did he actually mean when he said to himself that he had not experienced much? Did he mean by this travel, work, public service, sports, women? Of course he meant all of these things; yet, above all, women; because if his life was deficient in other spheres it certainly upset him, but he didn't have to lay the blame for it on himself; anyhow, not for work that was uninteresting and without prospects; not for curtailing his travels because he didn't have money or reliable party references; finally, not even for the fact that when he was twenty he had injured his knee and had had to give up sports, which he had enjoyed. On the other hand, the realm of women was for him a sphere of relative freedom, and that being so, he couldn't make any excuses about it; here he could have demonstrated his wealth; women became for him the one legitimate criterion of life's *density*.

But no such luck! Things had gone somewhat badly for him with women: Until he was twenty-five (though he was a good-looking guy) shyness would tie him up in knots; then he fell in love, got married, and after seven years had persuaded himself that it was possible to find the infinity of erotic possibilities in one woman; then he got divorced and the one-woman apologetics (and the illusion of infinity) melted away, and in their place came an agreeable taste for and boldness in the pursuit of women (a pursuit of their varied finiteness); unfortunately his bad financial situation frustrated his newfound desires (he had to pay his former wife for the support of a child he was allowed to see once or twice a year), and conditions in the small town were such that the curiosity of the neighbors was as enormous as the choice of women was scant.

And time was already passing very quickly, and all at once he was standing in the bathroom in front of the oval mirror located above the washbasin; in his right hand he held over his head a round mirror and was transfixed examining the bald spot that had begun to appear; this sight suddenly (without preparation) brought home to him the banal truth that what he'd missed couldn't be made good. He found himself in a state of chronic ill humor and was even assailed by thoughts of suicide. Naturally (and it is necessary to emphasize this, in order not to see him as a hysterical or stupid person), he appreciated the comic aspects of these thoughts, and he knew that he would never carry them out (he laughed inwardly at his own suicide note: *I won't put up with my bald spot. Farewell!*), but it is enough that these thoughts, however platonic they may have been, assailed him at all. Let us try to understand: the thoughts made themselves felt within him perhaps as the overwhelming desire to give up the race makes itself felt within a marathon runner, when halfway through he discovers that shamefully (and moreover through his own fault, his own blunders) he is losing. He also considered his race lost, and he didn't feel like running any farther.

And now he bent down over the small table and placed one cup of coffee on it in front of the couch (on which he was going to sit down), the other in front of the armchair, in which his visitor was sitting, and said to himself that there was a strange spitefulness in the fact that he had encountered this woman, with whom he had once been madly in love and whom he had allowed to escape him (through his own fault), encountered her precisely when he found himself in this state of mind and at a time when it was no longer possible to recapture anything.

4

She would hardly have guessed that in his eyes she was *the one who had escaped him*; still, she had always remembered the night they had spent together; she remembered how he had looked then (he was twenty, didn't know how to dress, used to blush, and his boyishness amused her); and she remembered what she had been like (she had been almost forty, and a thirst for beauty drove her into the arms of other men, but also drove her away from them; she had always thought that her life should have resembled a *delightful ball*, and she feared that her unfaithfulness to her husband might turn into an ugly habit).

Yes, she had decreed beauty for herself, as people decree moral injunctions for themselves; if she had noticed any ugliness in her own life, she would perhaps have fallen into despair. And because she was now aware that after fifteen years she must seem old to her host (with all the ugliness that this brings with it), she wanted quickly to unfold an imaginary fan in front of her face, and to this end she deluged him with questions: she asked him how he had come to this town; she asked him about his job; she complimented him on the coziness of his bachelor apartment, and praised the view from the window over the rooftops of the town (she said that it was of course no special view, but that there was an airiness and freedom about it). She named the painters of several framed reproductions of impressionist pictures (this was not difficult, in the apartments of most poor Czech intellectuals one was certain to find these cheap prints), then she got up from the table with her unfinished cup of coffee in her hand and bent over a small writing desk, on which were a few photographs in a stand (it didn't escape her that among them there was no photo of a young woman), and she asked whether the face of the old woman in one of them belonged to his mother (he confirmed this).

Then he asked her what she had meant when she

had told him earlier that she had come here to take care of some things. She really dreaded speaking about the cemetery (here on the sixth floor she not only felt high above the roofs, but also pleasantly high above her own life); when he insisted, though, she finally confessed (but very briefly, because the immodesty of hasty frankness had always been foreign to her) that she had lived here many years before, that her husband was buried here (she was silent about the cancellation of the grave), and that she and her son had been coming here for the last ten years without fail on All Souls' Day.

5

"Every year?" This statement saddened him, and once again he thought of the spitefulness of fate; if only he'd met her six years ago when he'd moved here, everything could have been possible; she wouldn't have been so marked by age, her appearance wouldn't have been so different from the image he had of the woman he had loved fifteen years before; it would have been within his power to surmount the difference and perceive both images (the image of the past and that of the present) as one. But now they stood hopelessly far apart.

She drank her coffee and talked. He tried hard to

determine precisely the extent of the transformation by means of which she was escaping him *for the second time*: her face was wrinkled (in vain did the layer of powder try to deny this); her neck was withered (in vain did the high collar try to hide this); her cheeks sagged; her hair (but it was almost beautiful!) had grown gray; however, her hands drew his attention most of all (unfortunately, it was not possible to touch them up with powder or paint): bunches of blue veins stood out on them, so that all at once they were the hands of a man.

In him pity was mixed with anger, and he felt like drowning their too-long-put-off meeting in alcohol; he asked her if she wanted some cognac (he had an opened bottle in the cabinet behind the screen); she replied that she didn't, and he remembered that even fifteen years before she had drunk almost not at all, perhaps so that alcohol wouldn't make her behave contrary to the demands of good taste and decorum. And when he saw the delicate movement of her hand with which she refused the offer of cognac, he realized that this charm, this magic, this grace, which had enraptured him, was still the same in her, though hidden beneath the mask of old age, and was in itself still attractive, even though it was behind a grille.

When it crossed his mind that this was *the grille of age,* he felt immense pity for her, and this pity brought her nearer to him (this woman who had once been so dazzling, before whom he used to be tongue-tied), and he wanted to have a conversation with her and to talk the way a friend talks with a friend, at length, in a blue atmosphere of melancholy resignation. He started to talk (and it did indeed turn into a long talk) and eventually he got to the pessimistic thoughts that had visited him of late. Naturally he was silent about the bald spot that was beginning to appear (it was just like her silence about the canceled grave); on the other hand the vision of the bald spot was transubstantiated into quasi-philosophical maxims to the effect that time passes more quickly than man is able to live, and that life is terrible, because everything in it is necessarily doomed to extinction; he voiced these and similar maxims, to which he awaited a sympathetic response; but he didn't get it.

"I don't like that kind of talk," she said almost vehemently. "Everything you've been saying is awfully superficial."

6

She didn't like conversations about growing old or dying, because they contained images of physical ugliness, which went against the grain with her. Several times, almost in a fluster, she repeated to her host that his opinions were *superficial*; after all, she said, a man is more than just a body that wastes away, a man's work is substantial and that is what he leaves behind for others. Her advocacy of this opinion wasn't new; it had first come to her aid when, thirty years earlier, she had fallen in love with her former husband, who was nineteen years older than she. She had never ceased to respect him wholeheartedly (in spite of all her infidelities, about which he either didn't know or didn't want to know), and she took pains to convince herself that her husband's intellect and importance would fully outweigh the heavy load of his years.

"What kind of work, I ask you? What kind of work do we leave behind?" protested her host with a bitter laugh.

She didn't want to refer to her dead husband, though she firmly believed in the lasting value of everything that he had accomplished; she therefore only said that every man accomplishes something, which in itself may be most modest, but that in this and only in this is his value; then she went on to talk about herself, how she worked in a house of culture in a suburb of Prague, how she organized lectures and poetry readings; she spoke (with an excitement that seemed out of proportion to him) about "the grateful faces" of the public; then she expatiated on how beautiful it was to have a son and to see her own features (her son looked like her) changing into the face of a man; how it was beautiful to give him everything that a mother can give a son and then to fade quietly into the background of his life.

It was not by chance that she had begun to talk

about her son, because all day her son had been in her thoughts, a reproachful reminder of the morning's failure at the cemetery; it was strange; she had never let any man impose his will on her, but her own son subjugated her, and she didn't understand how. The failure at the cemetery had upset her so much today, above all because she felt guilty before him and feared his reproaches. Of course she had long suspected that her son so jealously watched over the way she honored his father's memory (it was he who insisted every All Souls' Day that they should not fail to visit the cemetery!), not so much out of love for his dead father as from a desire to usurp his mother, to assign her to a widow's proper confines. For that's how it was, even if he never voiced it and she tried hard (without success) not to know it: the idea that his mother could still have a sex life disgusted him: everything in her that remained sexual (at least in the realm of possibility and chance) disgusted him, and because the idea of sex is connected with the idea of youthfulness, he was disgusted by everything that was still youthful in her; he was no longer a child, and his mother's youthfulness (combined with the aggressiveness of her motherly care) disagreeably thwarted his relationship with girls, who had begun to interest him; he wanted to have an old mother; only from such a mother would he tolerate love, and it was only such a mother he was capable of loving. And although at times she realized that in this way he was pushing her toward the grave, she had finally submitted to him, succumbed to his pressure, and even idealized her capitulation, persuading herself that the beauty of her life consisted precisely in quietly fading out in the shadow of another life. In the name of this idealization (without which the wrinkles on her face would have made her far more uneasy), she now conducted with such unexpected warmth this dispute with her host.

But her host suddenly leaned across the low table that stood between them, stroked her hand, and said: "Forgive my chatter. You know that I always was an idiot."

7

Their dispute didn't irritate him; on the contrary his visitor yet again confirmed her identity for him. In her protest against his pessimistic talk (wasn't this above all a protest against ugliness and bad taste?), he recognized her as the person he had once known, so her former appearance and their old adventure filled his thoughts all the more. Now he wished only that nothing destroy the intimate mood, so favorable to their conversation (for that reason he stroked her hand and called himself an idiot), and he wanted to tell her about the thing that seemed most important to him at this moment: their adventure together. For he was convinced that he had experienced something very special with her, which she didn't suspect and which he himself with difficulty would now try to put into precise words.

He no longer even remembered how they had met; apparently she sometimes came in contact with his student friends, but he remembered perfectly the out-of-the-way Prague café where they had been alone together for the first time: he had been sitting opposite her in a plush booth, depressed and silent, but at the same time thoroughly elated by her delicate hints that she was favorably disposed toward him. He had tried hard to visualize (without daring to hope for the fulfillment of these dreams) how she would look if he kissed her, undressed her, and made love to her—but he just couldn't manage it. Yes, there was something odd about it: He had tried a thousand times to imagine her in bed, but in vain. Her face kept on looking at him with its calm, gentle smile and he couldn't (even with the most dogged efforts of his imagination) distort it with the grimace of erotic ecstasy. *She absolutely escaped his imagination.*

And that was the situation, which had never since been repeated in his life. At that time he had stood face-to-face with the *unimaginable*. Obviously he was experiencing that very short period (the *paradisiac* period) when the imagination is not yet satiated by experience, has not become routine, knows little, and knows how to do little, so that the unimaginable still exists; and should the unimaginable become reality (without the mediation of the imaginable, without that narrow bridge of images), a man will be seized by panic and vertigo. Such vertigo did actually overtake him, when after several further meetings, in the course of which he hadn't resolved anything, she began to ask him in detail and with meaningful curiosity about his student room in the dormitory, so that she soon forced him to invite her there.

He had shared the little room in the dorm with another student, who for a glass of rum had promised not to return until after midnight; it bore little resemblance to his bachelor apartment of today: two metal cots, two chairs, a cupboard, a glaring, unshaded lightbulb, and frightful disorder. He tidied up the room, and at seven o'clock (it went with her refinement that she was habitually on time) she knocked on the door. It was September, and only gradually did it begin to get dark. They sat down on the edge of a cot and kissed. Then it got even darker, and he didn't want to switch on the light, because he was glad that he couldn't be seen, and hoped that the darkness would relieve the state of embarrassment in which he would find himself having to undress in front of her. (If he knew tolerably well how to unbutton women's blouses, he himself would undress in front of them with bashful haste.) This time, however, he didn't for a long time dare to undo her first button (it seemed to him that in the matter of beginning to undress there must exist some tasteful and elegant procedure, which only men who were experts knew, and he was afraid of betraying his inexperience), so that in the end she herself stood up and, asking with a smile, said: "Shouldn't I take off this armor?" She began to undress. It was dark, however, and he saw only the shadows of her movements. He hastily undressed too and gained some confidence only when they began (thanks to her patience) to make love. He looked into her face, but in the dusk her expression entirely eluded him, and he couldn't even make out her features. He regretted that it was dark, but it seemed impossible for him to get up and move away from her at that moment to turn on the switch by the door, so vainly he went on straining his eyes. But he didn't recognize her. It seemed to him that he was making love with someone else; with someone spurious or else someone quite unreal and unindividuated.

Then she had got on top of him (he could see only her raised shadow), and moving her hips, she said something in a muffled tone, in a whisper, but it wasn't clear whether she was talking to him or to herself. He couldn't make out the words and asked her what she had said. She went on whispering, and even when he clasped her to him again, he couldn't understand what she was saying.

8

She listened to her host and became increasingly absorbed in details she had long ago forgotten: for instance, in those days she used to wear a pale blue summer suit, in which, they said, she looked like an inviolable angel (yes, she recalled that suit); she used to wear a large ivory comb stuck in her hair, which they said gave her a majestically old-fashioned look; at the café she always used to order tea with rum (her only alcoholic vice), and all this pleasantly carried her away from the cemetery, away from the vanished monument, away from her sore feet, away from the house of culture, and away from the reproachful eyes of her son. Ah, she thought, whatever I am today, if a bit of my youth lives on in this man's memory, I haven't lived in vain. This immediately struck her as a new corroboration of her conviction that the worth of a human being lies in the ability to extend oneself, to go outside oneself, to exist in and for other people.

She listened and didn't resist him when from time to time he stroked her hand; the stroking merged with the soothing tone of the conversation and had a disarming indefiniteness about it (for whom was it intended? for the woman *about whom* he was speaking or for the woman *to whom* he was speaking?); after all, she liked the man who was stroking her; she even said to herself that she liked him better than the young man of fifteen years ago, whose boyishness, if she remembered correctly, had been rather a nuisance.

When he, in his account, got to the moment when her moving shadow had risen above him and he had vainly endeavored to understand her whispering, he fell silent for an instant, and she (foolishly, as if he could know those words and would want to remind her of them after so many years like some forgotten mystery) asked softly: "And what was I saying?"

9

"I don't know," he replied. He didn't know; at that time she had escaped not only his imagination but also his perceptions; she had escaped his sight and hearing. When he had switched on the light in the dormitory room, she was already dressed, everything about her was once again sleek, dazzling, perfect, and he vainly sought a connection between her face in the light and the face that a moment before he had been guessing at in the darkness. They hadn't parted yet, but he was already trying to remember her; he tried to imagine how her (unseen) face and (unseen) body had looked when they'd made love a little while before—but without success. She was still escaping his imagination.

He had made up his mind that next time he would make love to her with the light on. Only there wasn't a next time. From that day on she adroitly and tactfully avoided him. He had failed hopelessly, yet it wasn't clear why. They'd certainly made love beautifully, but he also knew how impossible he had been *beforehand*, and he was ashamed of this; he felt condemned by her avoidance and no longer dared to pursue her.

"Tell me, why did you avoid me then?"

"I beg you," she said in the gentlest of voices. "It was so long ago that I don't know." And when he pressed her further she protested: "You shouldn't always return to the past. It's enough that we have to devote so much time to it against our will." She said this only to ward off his insistence (and perhaps the last sentence, spoken with a light sigh, referred to her morning visit to the cemetery), but he perceived her statement differently: as an intense and purposeful clarification for him of the fact (this obvious thing) that there were not two women (from the past and from the present), but only one and the same woman, and that she, who had escaped him fifteen years earlier, was here now, was within reach of his hand.

"You're right, the present is more important," he said in a meaningful tone, and he looked intently at her face. She was smiling with her mouth half open, and he glimpsed a row of white teeth. At that instant a recollection flashed through his head: that time in his dorm room she had put his fingers into her mouth and bitten them hard until it had hurt. Meanwhile he had been feeling the whole inside of her mouth, and he distinctly remembered that on one side at the back her upper teeth were missing (this had not disgusted him at the time; on the contrary such a trivial imperfection went with her age, which attracted and aroused him). But now, looking into the space between her teeth and the corner of her mouth, he saw that her teeth were too strikingly white and that none were missing, and this made him shudder; once again she split apart into images of two women, but he didn't want to admit it; he wanted to reunite them by force and violence, and so said: "Don't you really feel like having some cognac?" When with a charming smile and a mildly raised eyebrow she shook her head, he went behind the screen, took out the bottle, put it to his lips, and took a swig. Then it occurred to him that she would be able to detect his secret action from his breath, and so he picked up two small glasses and the bottle and carried them into the room. Once more she shook her head. "At least symbolically," he said and filled both glasses. He clinked her glass and made a toast: "This is to talking about you only in the present tense!" He downed his drink, and she moistened her lips. He took a seat on the arm of her chair and seized her hands.

10

She hadn't suspected when she had agreed to go to his bachelor apartment that it could come to *such* touching, and at first she had been struck by fright; as if touching had come before she had been able to prepare herself (the *state of permanent preparedness* that is familiar to the mature woman she had lost long ago; we should perhaps find in this fright something akin to the fright of a very young girl who has just been kissed for the first time, for if the young girl is *not yet* and she, the visitor, was *no longer* prepared, then this "no longer" and "not yet" are mysteriously related as the peculiarities of old age and childhood are related). Then he moved her from the armchair to the couch, clasped her to him, and stroked her whole body, and in his arms she felt formlessly soft (yes, soft, because her body had long ago lost the sensuality that had once ruled it, the sensuality that had endowed her muscles with the rhythm of tensing and relaxation and with the activity of a hundred delicate movements).

But the moment of fright quickly melted in his embrace, and she, very far from the beauty she had once been, now reverted, with dizzying speed, to being that woman, reverted to that woman's feelings and to her consciousness, and retrieved the old self-confidence of an erotically experienced woman, and because this was a self-confidence long unfelt, she felt it now more intensely than ever before; her body, which a short while before had still been surprised, fearful, passive, and soft, revived and responded now with its own caresses, and she felt the distinctness and adeptness of these caresses, and it filled her with happiness; these caresses, the way she put her face to his body, the delicate movements with which her torso answered his embrace—she found all this not like something learned, something she knew how to do and was now performing with cool satisfaction, but like something essentially *her own*, with which she merged in intoxication and exaltation as she found her own familiar continent (ah, the continent of beauty!), from which she had been banished and to which she now returned in celebration.

Her son was now infinitely far away; when her host had clasped her, in a corner of her mind she caught sight of the boy warning her of the danger, but then he quickly disappeared, and there remained only she and the man who was stroking and embracing her. But when he placed his lips on her lips and tried to open her mouth with his tongue, everything changed: she woke up. She firmly clenched her teeth (she felt her denture pressed against the roof of her mouth, she felt that her mouth had been filled), and she gently pushed him away, saying: "No. Really, please, I'd rather not."

When he kept on insisting, she held him by the wrists and repeated her refusal; then she said (it was hard for her to speak, but she knew that she must speak if she wanted him to obey her) that it was too late for them to make love; she reminded him of her age, if they did make love he would be disgusted with her and she would feel wretched about it, because what he had told her about the two of them was for her immensely beautiful and important. Her body was mortal and wasted, but she now knew that of it there still remained something incorporeal, something like the glow that shines even after a star has burned out; it didn't matter that she was growing old if her youth remained intact, present within another being. "You've erected a monument to me within your memory. We cannot allow it to be destroyed. Please understand me," she said, warding him off. "Don't let it happen. No, don't let it happen!"

11

He assured her that she was still beautiful, that in fact nothing had changed, that a human being always remains the same, but he knew that he was deceiving her and that she was right: he was well aware of his physical supersensitivity, his increasing fastidiousness about the external defects of a woman's body, which in recent years had driven him to ever younger and therefore, as he bitterly realized, also ever emptier and stupider women; yes, there was no doubt about it: if he got her to make love it would end in disgust, and this disgust would then splatter with mud not only the present, but also the image of the beloved woman of long ago, an image cherished like a jewel in his memory.

He knew all this, but only intellectually, and the intellect meant nothing in the face of this desire, which knew only one thing: the woman he had thought of as unattainable and elusive for fifteen years was here; at last he could see her in broad daylight, at last he might discern from her body of today what her body had been like then, from her face of today what her face had been like then. Finally he might read the unimaginable expression on her face while making love.

He clasped her shoulders and looked into her eyes: "Don't fight me. It's absurd to fight me."

12

But she shook her head, because she knew that it wasn't absurd for her to refuse him; she knew men and their approach to the female body; she was aware that in love even the most passionate idealism will not rid the body's surface of its terrible, basic importance; it is true that she still had a nice figure, which had preserved its original proportions, and especially in her clothes she looked quite youthful; but she knew that when she undressed she would expose the wrinkles in her neck, the long scar from stomach surgery ten years before.

And just as the consciousness of her present physical appearance, which she had forgotten a short while before, returned to her, so there arose from the street below (until now, this room had seemed to her safely high above her life) the anxieties of the morning; they were filling the room, they were alighting on the prints behind glass, on the armchair, on the table, on the empty coffee cup—and her son's face dominated their procession; when she caught sight of it, she blushed and fled somewhere deep inside herself; foolishly she had been on the point of wishing to escape from the path he had assigned to her and which she had trodden up to now with a smile and words of enthusiasm; she had been on the point of wishing (at least for a moment) to escape, and now she must obediently return and admit that it was the only path suitable for her. Her son's face was so derisive that, in shame, she felt herself growing smaller and smaller before him until, humiliated, she turned into the mere scar on her stomach.

Her host held her by the shoulders and once again repeated: "It's absurd for you to fight me," and she shook her head, but quite mechanically, because what she was seeing was not her host but the face of her son-enemy, whom she hated the more the smaller and the more humiliated she felt. She heard him reproaching her about the canceled grave, and now, from the chaos of her memory, illogically there surged forth the sentence she had shouted at his face with rage: *The old dead must make room for the young dead, my boy!*

13

He didn't have the slightest doubt that this would actually end in disgust, for even now the look he fixed on her (a searching and penetrating look) was not free from a certain disgust, but the curious thing was that he didn't mind; on the contrary, it aroused him and goaded him on as if he were wishing for this disgust: the desire for coition approached the desire for disgust; the desire to read on her body what he had for so long been unable to know mingled with the desire immediately to soil the newly deciphered secret.

Where did this passion come from? Whether he realized it or not, a unique opportunity was presenting itself: to him his visitor embodied everything that he had never had, that had escaped him, that he had missed, everything that by its absence made his present age intolerable, with his thinning hair, his dismally meager balance sheet; and he, whether he realized it or only vaguely suspected it, could now strip all these pleasures that had been denied him of their significance and color (for it was precisely their terrific colorfulness that made his life

so sadly colorless), he could reveal that they were worthless, that they were only appearances doomed to destruc-
tion, that they were only metamorphosed dust; he could
take revenge upon them, demean them, destroy them.

"Don't fight me," he repeated as he tried to draw her
close.

14

Before her eyes she still saw her son's derisive face, and
when now her host drew her to him by force she said,
"Please, leave me alone for a minute," and she escaped
his embrace; she didn't want to interrupt what was rac-
ing through her head: the old dead must make room for
the young dead and monuments were useless, even her
monument, which this man beside her had honored for
fifteen years in his thoughts, was useless, all monuments were useless. That is what she silently said to her
son. And with vengeful delight she watched his con-
torted face and heard him shout: "You never talked
like this before, Mother!" Of course she knew that she
had never spoken like this, but this moment was filled
with a light, under which everything became quite different.

There was no reason why she should give preference
to monuments over life; her own monument had a single

meaning for her: that at this moment she could abuse it for the sake of her disparaged body; the man who was sitting beside her appealed to her; he was young and very likely (almost certainly) he was the last man who would appeal to her and whom, at the same time, she could have, and that alone was important; if he then became disgusted with her and destroyed her monument in his thoughts, it made no difference because her monument was outside her, just as his thoughts and memory were outside her, and everything that was outside her made no difference. "You never talked like this before, Mother!" She heard her son's cry, but she paid no attention to him. She was smiling.

"You're right, why should I fight you?" she said quietly, and she got up. Then she slowly began to unbutton her dress. Evening was still a long way off. This time the room was filled with light.

Dr. Havel After Twenty Years

1

When Dr. Havel was leaving for a cure at a spa, his beautiful wife had tears in her eyes. She had them there out of compassion (some time ago he had been stricken with gall bladder attacks, and until that time she had never seen him sick), but she also had them there because the coming three weeks of separation aroused jealous anguish in her.

What? Could this actress—admired, beautiful, so many years younger than he—be jealous of an aging gentleman who in recent months had not left the house without slipping into his pocket a small bottle of tablets to relieve his insidious pains?

That, however, was the case, and no one understood her. Not even Dr. Havel, for she seemed to him invulnerably supreme, judging by her appearance. It had charmed him all the more when he had begun to know her better several years before and discovered her simplicity, her homebodiness, and her shyness; it was curious: even after they were married, the actress altogether disregarded the advantages of her youth; it was as if she was bewitched by love and by her husband's formidable reputation as a womanizer, so that he seemed to her to always be elusive and unfathomable, and even though he tried to convince her every

197

day with infinite patience (and absolute sincerity) that he did not have and never would have anyone but her, she was still bitterly and madly jealous; only her natural refinement kept a lid on this nasty feeling, but it continued to bubble up even more.

Havel knew all this; at times it moved him, at times it angered him, and sometimes it wearied him, but because he loved his wife he did everything to relieve her anguish. This time again he made an attempt to help her: he greatly exaggerated his pain and the dangerous state of his health, for he knew that the fear his wife felt because of his illness was uplifting and comforting to her, whereas the fear inspired in her by his health (a fear of infidelities and pitfalls) wore her down; he often talked about Dr. Frantiska, who was going to treat him at the spa; the actress knew her, and the thought of her physical appearance, completely benign and absolutely alien to any lecherous ideas, reassured her.

When Dr. Havel was seated in the bus, looking at the tearful eyes of the beauty standing on the sidewalk, to tell the truth he felt relieved, for her love was not only sweet but also oppressive. Once at the spa he didn't feel so well. After partaking of the mineral waters, which he had to do three times a day and which went right through his body, he had pains and felt tired. And when he met good-looking women in the colonnade, with dismay he found that he felt old and didn't desire them. The only woman whom he had been granted among the boundless number was the good Frantiska, who jabbed injections into him, took his blood pressure, prodded his stomach, and supplied him with information about what was going on at the spa and about her two children, especially her son, who, she said, looked like her.

This was his state of mind when he received a letter from his wife. Ah, alas, this time her refinement had kept poor watch over her passionate jealousy; the letter was full of grievances and complaints; she said she didn't want to reproach him with anything, but that she hadn't slept the whole night; she said she well knew that her love was a burden to him, and she was able to imagine how happy he was now that he was away from her and could rest a bit; yes, she understood how much she irritated him, and she also knew that she was too weak to change his life, which was always to be besieged by hordes of women; yes she knew it, she didn't protest against it, but she cried and couldn't sleep. . . .

When Dr. Havel had read through this list of laments, he recalled the three years during which he had tried patiently but in vain to portray himself to his wife as a reformed libertine and a loving husband; he felt immense weariness and hopelessness. In anger he crumpled up the letter and threw it into the wastebasket.

2

The following day he felt a little better; his gall bladder no longer hurt at all, and he felt a slight but unmistakable desire for several of the women whom he had seen walking through the colonnade in the morning. This small gain was, however, wiped out by his recognition of something far worse: these women passed him by without the least show of interest; to them he blended into the ailing parade of pale mineral-water sippers.

"You see, it's getting better," said Dr. Frantiska, after prodding him that morning. "But stick strictly to the diet. The women patients you run into at the colonnade are fortunately rather old and sick, so they shouldn't bother you, and for you it's better that way, because above all you need to rest."

Havel was tucking his shirt into his pants; he was standing in front of a small mirror hanging in a corner above the washbasin and bitterly examining his face. Then he said very sadly: "You're wrong. I clearly noticed that among the majority of old women there was a minority of quite pretty women strolling through the colonnade. Only they didn't spare me so much as a glance."

"I'll believe anything you like, but not that," the woman doctor replied, and Dr. Havel, having torn his eyes away from the sad spectacle in the mirror, peered into her unquestioning, loyal eyes. He felt much gratitude toward her, even though he knew she was only expressing belief in a tradition, belief in the role she had become accustomed to seeing him play: a role of which she disapproved (but always softheartedly).

Then someone knocked at the door. When Frantiska opened it a little, the head of a young man, nodding in greeting, could be seen. "Ah, it's you! I'd completely forgotten!" She asked the young man to come into the consulting room and explained to Havel: "This is the editor of the spa magazine; he's been looking for you for the past two days."

The young man began to apologize at length for disturbing Dr. Havel at such an awkward time, and tried to take on a facetious air (unfortunately it turned out somewhat forced and unpleasantly strained). He said that Dr. Havel should not be angry with Dr. Frantiska for betraying his presence here, for the editor would have caught up with him anyway, maybe even in the bathtub with the carbonic water, and also that Dr. Havel should not be angry at his audacity, for this attribute was one of the necessities of the journalistic profession and without it, he wouldn't be able to earn his living. Then he became talkative about the illustrated magazine, which the spa put out once a month, and he explained that in every issue there was an interview with some prominent patient taking the cure. He mentioned a few names, among them a member of the government, a woman singer, and a hockey player.

"You see," said Frantiska, "the beautiful women at the colonnade haven't shown an interest in you; on the other hand you interest journalists."

"That's an awful step down," said Havel. He was, however, quite pleased with this interest, and he smiled at the editor, refusing his proposal with touchingly transparent insincerity: "I, my dear sir, am neither a member of the government nor a hockey player, and even less a woman singer. And although I don't want to underestimate my scientific research, it interests experts rather than the general public."

"But I don't want to interview you; that didn't even occur to me," replied the young man with prompt sincerity. "I want to talk with your wife. I've heard that she's going to visit you here."

"Then you're better informed than I," said Havel rather coldly; he then approached the mirror again and looked at his face; it didn't please him. He buttoned the top button of his shirt and kept silent while the young editor became embarrassed and lost his avowed journalistic audacity; he apologized to the woman doctor, he apologized to Dr. Havel, and he was glad to be leaving.

3

The journalist was scatterbrained rather than stupid. He didn't think much of the spa magazine, but, being as its sole editor, every month he had to do the things necessary to fill the twenty-four pages with the requisite photographs and words. In the summer it was tolerably easy, because the spa teemed with prominent guests, various orchestras took turns at the open-air concerts, and there was no lack of gossip items. On the other hand in the damp and cold months the colonnade was filled with countrywomen and boredom, so he couldn't let an opportunity escape him. When yesterday he had heard somewhere that the husband of a well-known actress was taking a cure here, the husband of the very one who was appearing in the new detective film that was currently and successfully distracting the gloomy spa guests, he began immediately to hunt for him.

But now he was ashamed.

He was always unsure of himself and for this reason slavishly dependent on the people with whom he came in contact. It was in their sight and judgment that he timidly found out what he was like and how much he was worth. Now he concluded that the had been found wretched, stupid, and tiresome, and he took this all the more to heart because at first sight he had rather liked the man who had so judged him. And so he uneasily telephoned the woman doctor the same day to ask her who in fact the actress's husband was, and learned that he was not only a top physician but was also very famous in other ways too; had the editor really never heard of him?

The editor confessed that he hadn't, and the woman doctor indulgently said: "Well, of course, you're still a child. And fortunately you're an ignoramus in the field in which Havel has excelled."

When more questions to more people revealed that

the field was erotic knowledge, in which Dr. Havel was said to have no competition in his native land, the editor was mortified to have been called an ignoramus, and even to have confirmed this by never having heard of Havel. And because he had always longingly dreamed of someday being an expert like this man, it bothered him that he had acted like a disagreeable fool precisely in front of him, in front of his master. He remembered his own chatter, his silly jokes, his lack of tact, and he humbly had to agree that the verdict he read in the master's disapproving silence and absentminded look into the mirror was justified.

The spa town in which this story takes place is not large and people meet one another several times a day, whether they want to or not. And so it wasn't difficult for the young editor soon to come across the man he was thinking about. It was late afternoon, and a crowd of gall bladder sufferers was slowly moving among the pillars of the colonnade. Dr. Havel was sipping the smelly water from a porcelain mug and grimacing slightly. The young editor went up to him and began confusedly to apologize. He had never suspected, he said, that the husband of the well-known actress was he, Dr. Havel, and not a different Havel; in Bohemia there were many Havels, and unfortunately the actress's husband had not been associated in the editor's mind with that famous doctor, about whom the editor had, of course, long ago heard, and not only as a top physician, but—perhaps he might venture to say it—also on account of the most varied rumors and anecdotes.

There's no denying that the young man's words pleased Dr. Havel in his ill-humored state of mind, especially the remarks about the rumors, for Havel well knew that they were subject, like man himself, to the laws of aging and extinction.

"You don't need to apologize," he said to the young man, and because he saw the editor's embarrassment, he took him gently by the arm and got him to take a stroll through the colonnade. "Anyhow, it's not worth talking about," he consoled him. At the same time, though, he himself dwelled on the apology and several times said: "So you've heard about me?" and each time laughed happily.

"Yes," the editor eagerly assented. "But I didn't imagine you at all like this."

"Well, how did you imagine me?" asked Dr. Havel with genuine interest, and when the editor stammered something, not knowing what to say, Havel said gloomily: "I know. Unlike real people the characters in stories, legends, and anecdotes are made of a substance not subject to the corruption of age. No, by this I don't mean to say that legends and anecdotes are immortal, certainly they too age, and with them their characters, only they grow old in such a way that their appearance does not change and deteriorate but pales slowly, becomes transparent, and eventually merges with the transparency of space. So in the end Pepe le Moko disappears as well as Havel the Collector, and also Moses and Pallas Athena and Saint Francis of Assisi. But consider that Francis will slowly grow pale, and with him the little birds that are sitting on his shoulder, and the fawn that rubs against his leg, and the grove of olive trees that provides him with shade; consider that his whole landscape will become transparent with him, and together they will slowly turn into comforting azure, while I, my dear friend, just as I am, naked, torn out of a legend, am going to vanish against the background of an implacably garish landscape and before the eyes of derisive, living youth."

Havel's speech puzzled and excited the young man, and they kept on walking together for a long time through the deepening dusk. When they parted Havel declared that he was tired of his diet and that tomorrow he would like to go out for a good dinner; he asked the editor if he would like to accompany him.

Of course the young man accepted the invitation.

4

"Don't tell my doctor," said Havel, when he had taken a seat across the table from the editor and picked up the menu, "but I have my own conception of a diet: I strictly avoid all the foods I don't enjoy." Then he asked the young man what aperitif he would have.

The editor was not used to drinking aperitifs before

dinner, and because nothing else occurred to him, he said: "Vodka."

Dr. Havel looked displeased: "Vodka stinks of the Russian soul."

"That's true," said the editor, and from that moment he was lost. He was like a student at the final high school oral examination before his committee. He didn't try to say what he thought and do what he wanted, but attempted to satisfy the examiners; he tried to divine their thoughts, their whims, their taste; he wanted to be worthy of them. Not for anything in the world would he have admitted that his meals were usually poor and rudimentary, and that he didn't have a clue about which wine went with which meat. And Dr. Havel unwittingly tormented him when he persisted in conferring with him about the choice of hors d'oeuvre, main course, wine, and cheese.

When the editor realized that the committee had taken off many points in the gastronomy examination, he wanted more than ever to make up the loss, and now in the interval between the hors d'oeuvre and the main course, he conspicuously looked around at the women in the restaurant and by various remarks tried hard to demonstrate his interest and experience. But once again he was the loser. When he said that the red-haired woman sitting two tables away would certainly be an excellent mistress, Dr. Havel without malice asked him what made him say that. The editor replied vaguely, and when the doctor asked about his experiences with redheads, he became entangled in improbable lies and soon fell silent.

By contrast Dr. Havel felt happy and relaxed with the editor's admiring eyes fixed on him. He ordered a bottle of red wine with the meat, and the young man, encouraged by the alcohol, made a further attempt to become worthy of the master's favor; he commented at length about a girl he had recently met and whom he had been wooing for the past several weeks, with, he said, great hope of success. His statement was not too substantial, and the unnatural smile that covered his face and was intended, with its artificial ambiguity, to state what he had left unsaid, only conveyed that he was trying to overcome his insecurity. Havel was well aware of all this and, moved by pity, asked the editor about the most diverse physical attributes of the girl, so as to detain him on this agreeable topic for as long as possible and give him a chance to talk more freely. However, even this time the young man was an incredible failure: it turned out that he wasn't able to describe with sufficient precision the general architecture of the girl's body or particular features of it, and even less the girl's mind. And so Dr. Havel himself finally talked expansively and, becoming elated by the coziness of the evening and by the wine, overwhelmed the editor with a witty monologue of his own reminiscences, anecdotes, and remarks.

The editor sipped his wine, listened, and at the same time experienced ambiguous emotions. On the one hand he was unhappy: he felt his own insignificance and stupidity, he felt like a questionable apprentice in front of an unquestionable master, and he was ashamed to open his mouth; but at the same time he was also happy: it flattered him that the master was sitting opposite him, having a nice, long, friendly chat with him and confiding to him the most varied, intimate, and valuable observations.

When Havel's speech had already lasted too long, the young man yearned, after all, to open his own mouth, to make his own contribution, to join in, to prove his ability to be a partner; he spoke, therefore, once more about his girl and invited Havel to take a look at her the next day and let him know how she looked to him in the light of his experience; put differently (yes, in his whimsical frame of mind he used these words), to *check her out.*

What was he thinking of? Was it only an involuntary notion born of wine and the intense desire to say something?

However spontaneous the idea may have been, the editor was pursuing at least a threefold benefit:

—by means of the conspiracy involving a common and clandestine judgment (the checking out), a secret bond would be established between him and the master, they would become real pals, a thing the editor craved;

—if the master voiced his approval (and the young man expected this, for he himself was greatly taken with the girl in question), this would be approval of the young man, of his judgment and taste, so that in the master's eyes he would change from an apprentice into a journeyman, and in his own eyes he would also be more important than before;

—and last: the girl would then mean more to the young man than before, and the pleasure he experienced in her presence would change from fictional to real (for the young man occasionally realized that the world in which he lived was for him a labyrinth of values, whose worth he only quite dimly surmised; therefore he knew that illusory values could become real values only when they were *endorsed*).

5

When Dr. Havel awoke the next day he felt a slight pain in his gall bladder because of yesterday's dinner; and when he looked at his watch he found that in half an hour he had to be at a hydrotherapy session and would therefore have to hurry, which of all things in life he liked to do least; and when, combing his hair, he caught sight of his face in the mirror, it didn't please him. The day was beginning badly.

He didn't even have time for breakfast (he considered this a bad sign as well), and he hurried to the building that housed the baths. There was a long corridor with many doors; he knocked on one and a pretty blonde in a white smock peeped out; she ill-humoredly chided him for being late and asked him in. A moment after Dr. Havel went behind a screen in a cubicle to undress, he heard, "Will you hurry up?" The masseuse's voice became more and more impolite; it offended Havel and provoked him to retaliate (and alas, over the years Dr. Havel had become accustomed to only one way of retaliating against women!). He took off his underpants, pulled in his stomach, stuck out his chest, and was about to step out of the cubicle; but then, disgusted by an act that was beneath his dignity and that would have seemed ridiculous to him in someone else; he comfortably relaxed his stomach again and, with a nonchalance he considered worthy of his dignity, headed toward the large bath and immersed himself in the tepid water.

The masseuse, completely disregarding both his chest and his stomach, meanwhile turned several faucets on a large control board and, when Dr. Havel was already lying stretched out on the bottom of the bath, she seized his right foot under the water and put the nozzle of a hose, from which there issued a stinging stream, against his sole. Dr. Havel, who was ticklish, jerked his foot, so that the masseuse had to rebuke him.

It would certainly not have been too difficult to get the blonde to abandon her cold and impolite tone by means of some joke, gossip, or facetious question, only Havel was too angry and insulted for that. He said to himself that the blonde deserved to be punished and shouldn't have things made easy for her. As she ran the hose over his groin and he covered his genitals with his hands so that the stinging stream wouldn't hurt them, he asked her what she was doing that evening. Without looking at him, she asked him why he wanted to know. He explained to her that he was staying alone in a single bedroom and that he wanted her to come to him there that evening. "Maybe you've confused me with someone else," said the blonde, and she told him to turn over onto his stomach.

And so Dr. Havel lay with his stomach on the bottom of the bath, holding his chin up high so that he could breathe. He felt the stinging stream massaging his calves, and he was satisfied with the way he had addressed the masseuse. Dr. Havel had for a long time been in the habit of punishing rebellious, insolent, or spoiled women by leading them over to his couch coldly, without any tenderness, almost without a word, and also by then dismissing them in an equally chilly manner. Only after a moment did it occur to him that though he had no doubt addressed the masseuse with appropriate coldness and without any sort of tenderness, still he had not led her to the couch and was not likely to do so. He understood that he had been rejected and that this was a new insult. For this reason he was glad when at last he was drying himself with a towel in the cubicle.

He quickly left the building and hurried to the Time Cinema to look at the display case; three publicity stills were displayed there, and in one of them his wife was kneeling in terror over a corpse. Dr. Havel looked at that sweet face, distorted by fright, and felt boundless love and boundless yearning. For a long time he couldn't drag himself away from the display case. Then he decided to drop in on Frantiska.

6

"Get me long distance, please, I have to talk to my wife," he said to her when she had seen her patient out and asked him into the consulting room.

"Has something happened?"

"Yes," said Havel. "I feel lonely!"

Frantiska looked at him mistrustfully, dialed the long-distance operator, and gave the number Havel told her. Then she hung up and said: "So you're lonely?"

"And why shouldn't I be?" Havel said angrily. "You're like my wife. You see in me someone whom I haven't been for a long time. I'm humble, I'm forlorn, I'm sad. The years weigh heavily on me. And I'm telling you that this is not a pleasant thing."

"You should have children," the woman doctor replied. "Then you wouldn't think so much about yourself. The years also weigh heavily on me, but I don't think about it. When I see my son growing up, I look forward to seeing what he will be like as a man, and I don't complain about the passage of time. Imagine what he said to me yesterday: 'Why,' he said, 'are there doctors in the world when everyone will die anyway?' What do you say to that? What would you have said to him?"

Luckily Dr. Havel didn't have time to answer because the telephone rang. He picked up the receiver, and when he heard his wife's voice, he immediately blurted out how sad he was, how he had no one to talk to or look at here, how he couldn't bear it alone here.

Through the receiver a small voice was heard, distrustful at first, startled, almost faltering, which under the impact of her husband's words unbent a little.

"Please, come here to see me; come to see me as soon as you can!" said Havel, and heard his wife reply that she'd like to but that nearly every day she had a show to do.

"Nearly every day isn't every day," said Havel, and he heard his wife say that she had the following day free, but that she didn't know if it was worth coming for just one day.

"How can you say that? Don't you realize how precious one day is in this short life of ours?"

"And you really aren't angry with me?" asked the small voice into the receiver.

"Why should I be angry?"

"Because of that letter. You're in pain, and I bore you stiff with the silly letter of a jealous woman."

Dr. Havel murmured sweet nothings into the mouthpiece, and his wife (in a voice already grown quite tender) declared that she would come the next day.

214

"Whatever you say, I envy you," said Frantiska, when Havel had hung up the receiver. "You have everything. Girls at your beck and call and a happy marriage besides."

Havel looked at his friend, who talked to him of envy, but because of the very goodness of her heart, probably wasn't capable of that emotion. And he felt sorry for her, for he knew that the pleasure to be had from children cannot compensate for other pleasures, and, moreover, a pleasure burdened with the obligation to substitute for other pleasures will soon become too wearisome a pleasure.

He then left for lunch. After lunch he slept, and when he woke up he remembered that the young editor was awaiting him in a café, to present his girl to him. So he dressed and went out. As he walked down the stairs of the patients' building, in the hall near the cloakroom he caught sight of a tall woman who resembled a beautiful riding horse. Ah, this should not have happened! That is to say Havel always found precisely this type of woman madly attractive. The cloakroom attendant was handing the tall woman her coat, and Dr. Havel ran over to help her into it. The woman who resembled a horse casually thanked him, and Havel said: "Is there anything else I can do for you?" He was smiling at her, but she replied, without a smile, that he couldn't, and she dashed out of the building.

Dr. Havel felt as if he'd been slapped in the face, and in a renewed state of gloom he headed toward the café.

7

The editor had already been sitting in a booth beside his girlfriend for quite a while (he'd picked a place from which the entrance was visible), and he wasn't up to concentrating on conversation, which at other times used to bubble up between them gaily and unflaggingly. He was shy at the thought of Havel's arrival. For the first time today he had attempted to look at his girlfriend with a more critical eye. And while she was saying something (fortunately she went on saying something, so that the young man's inner anxiety remained unnoticed), he discovered several minor flaws in her beauty. This greatly disturbed him, even if in no time he was assuring himself that these minor flaws in fact made her beauty more interesting and that it was precisely these things that gave him a warm feeling of closeness to her whole being.

That is to say he loved the girl.

But if he loved her, why had he proceeded with this venture that would be so humiliating to her, *checking her out* with the lubricious doctor? And if we grant him extenuating circumstances, allowing that this was only a game for him, how was it that he had become so shy and troubled by a mere game?

This was not a game. The young man really did not know what his girl was like, he wasn't able to pass judgment on the degree of her beauty and attractiveness.

But was he really so naive and inexperienced that he

could not distinguish a pretty woman from an ugly one?

Not at all. The young man wasn't so inexperienced; he had already known a few women and had affairs with them, but while they were going on he had been concentrating far more on himself than on them. Take a look at this noteworthy detail: the young man recalled precisely when and how he had been dressed with which woman; he knew on what occasion he had worn pants that were too wide and had been unhappy about this; he knew that at another time he had worn a white sweater in which he had felt like a stylish sports-man, but he had no idea how his girlfriends had been dressed.

Yes, this is noteworthy: during his brief adventures he had undertaken long and detailed studies of himself in the mirror, while he had only an overall, general impression of his female counterparts; it was far more important to him how he himself was seen in the eyes of his partner than how she appeared to him. By this I don't mean to say that it didn't matter to him whether the girl he was seeing was or was not beautiful. It did matter. For he himself was not merely seen by the eyes of his partner, but both of them together were seen and judged by the eyes of others (by the eyes of the world), and it was very important to him that the world should be pleased with his girl, for he knew that through her was judged his choice, his taste, his status, thus he him-self. But precisely because what concerned him was the judgment of others, he had not dared to rely on his own eyes; until now, on the contrary, he had considered it sufficient to listen to the voice of general opinion and to accept it.

But what was the voice of general opinion against the voice of a master and an expert? The editor was looking anxiously toward the entrance, and when at last he caught sight of Dr. Havel's figure in the glass door, he pretended to be astonished and said to the girl that by sheer chance a certain distinguished man, whom he wanted to interview for his magazine within the next few days, was just coming in. He went to meet Havel and led him over to their table. The girl, interrupted for a moment by the introduction, soon picked up the thread of her incessant conversation and continued to chatter away.

Dr. Havel, rejected ten minutes before by the woman who resembled a riding horse, looked slowly at the prattling girl and sank deeper and deeper into a surly mood. The girl wasn't a beauty, but she was quite cute, and there was no doubt that Dr. Havel (who was alleged to be like death, because he took everything) would have taken her gladly any time. She possessed several features indicative of a curious, aesthetic ambiguity: At the base of her nose she had a shower of freckles, which could be taken as a flaw in the whiteness of her complexion, but also conversely as a natural gem; she was very slender, which could be taken as the inadequate filling out of ideal feminine proportions, but also conversely as the provocative delicacy of the child continuing to exist within the woman; she was immensely talkative, which could be taken as inconvenient blather, but also conversely as a useful trait, which would allow her partner to give himself up to his own thoughts in the shelter of her words whenever he liked and without fear of being caught.

The editor secretly and anxiously examined the doctor's face, and when it seemed to him that it was dangerously (and for his hopes unfavorably) lost in thought, he called over a waiter and ordered three cognacs. The girl protested that she did not drink, and then again slowly let herself be persuaded that she could drink and should, and Dr. Havel sadly realized that this aesthetically ambiguous creature, revealing in her stream of words all the simplicity of her inward nature, would very probability be, if he were to make a play for her, his third failure of the day. For he, Dr. Havel, once as supreme as death, was no longer the man he once had been.

Then the waiter brought the cognacs, they all three raised them to clink glasses, and Dr. Havel looked into the girl's blue eyes as into the hostile eyes of someone who was not going to belong to him. And when he understood the significance of these eyes as hostile, he reciprocated with hostility, and suddenly saw before him a creature aesthetically quite unambiguous: a sickly girl, her face splattered with a smudge of freckles, insufferably garrulous.

Even if this change, together with the young man's

gaze fixed on him with an anxious and questioning look, gratified Havel, this pleasure was small in comparison with the bitterness that left a gaping hole inside him. It occurred to Havel that he ought not to prolong this meeting, which could not bring him any pleasure; so he quickly took over the conversation, uttered several charming witticisms for the young man and the girl, expressed his satisfaction at having been able to spend an agreeable moment with them, stated that he had to be somewhere, and took his leave.

When the doctor reached the glass door, the young man tapped his forehead and told the girl that he had completely forgotten to make an appointment with the doctor about the interview. He rushed out of the booth and only caught up with Havel in the street. "Well, what do you say about her?" he asked.

Dr. Havel stared for a long while into the eyes of the young man, whose imploring look cheered him up.

On the other hand, Havel's silence chilled the editor, so that he began to retreat beforehand: "I know she isn't a beauty. . . ."

Havel said: "No, she isn't a beauty."

The editor lowered his head: "She talks a little too much. But aside from that, she's nice!"

"Yes, that girl is really nice," said Havel. "But a dog, a canary, or a duckling waddling about in a farmyard can also be nice. In life, my friend, it's not a question of having the greatest number of women, because that's too superficial a success. Rather, it's a question of cultivating one's own demanding taste, because in it is mirrored the extent of one's personal worth. Remember, my friend, that a real fisherman throws the little fish back into the water."

The young man began to apologize and declared that he himself had considerable doubts about the girl, which was borne out by the fact that he had asked Havel for his judgment.

"It's not important," said Havel.

But the young man went on apologizing and justifying himself, and he pointed out that in the fall there is a dearth of beautiful women in the spa town and a man has to put up with what there is.

"I don't agree with you in this matter," Havel replied. "I've seen several extremely attractive women here. But I'll tell you something. There exists a certain superficial prettiness in women, which small-town taste mistakenly considers beauty. And then there exists the genuine erotic beauty of women. Of course, it's not easy to recognize this at a mere glance. It is an art." Then he shook the young man's hand and left.

8

The editor fell into a terrible state: he understood that he was an incorrigible fool, lost in the unbounded (yes, it seemed to him unbounded) wilderness of his own youth; he realized that he had fallen in Dr. Havel's esteem, and he had discovered beyond a shadow of a doubt that his girl was uninteresting, insignificant, and not beautiful. When he sat down again beside her in the booth, it seemed to him that all the clientele at the café as well as the two busy waiters knew this and felt maliciously sorry for him. He called for the check and explained to the girl that he had pressing work to do and had to leave. The girl became downcast, and the young man's heart was wrung with grief. Even though he knew that he was throwing her back into the water like a real fisherman, deep down he still (secretly and with a kind of shame) loved her.

The next morning did not bring any light into his gloomy mood, and when he saw Dr. Havel walking toward him with a fashionably dressed woman, he felt within himself an envy akin almost to hatred. This lady was too blatantly beautiful and Dr. Havel's mood, as he nodded gaily to the editor, was too blatantly buoyant, so that the young man felt even more wretched.

"This is the editor of the local magazine; he made my acquaintance only so that he could meet you."

When the young man learned that before him was a woman he had seen on the movie screen, his insecurity increased even more; Havel forced him to walk with them, and the editor, because he didn't know what to say, began to explain his projected interview and supplemented it with a new idea: he said that he would do a double interview with Mrs. Havel and the doctor.

"But my dear friend," Havel admonished him, "the

conversations that we engaged in were pleasant and, thanks to you, also interesting. But tell me, why should we make them public in a periodical destined for gall bladder sufferers and people with duodenal ulcers?"

"I can easily imagine those conversations of yours," said Mrs. Havel smiling.

"We talked about women," said Dr. Havel. "In this gentleman here I found an excellent partner and debater for this subject, a bright companion in my dreary, dark days."

Mrs. Havel turned to the young man. "He didn't bore you?"

The editor was delighted that the doctor had called him his bright companion, and, once again, his envy was mingled with devoted gratitude. He declared that perhaps rather it was he who had bored the doctor; that is, he was too well aware of his inexperience and color-lessness, yes—he even added—of his worthlessness.

"Ah, my dear," said the actress, with a laugh, "you must have done a lot of showing off!"

The editor stood up for the doctor: "That's not true! You, my dear lady, don't know what a small town is like, what this backwater where I live is like."

"But it's beautiful here," protested the actress.

"Yes, for you, because you've come here just for a while. But I live here and will go on living here. Always the same circle of people, whom I already know only too well. Always the same people, who all think alike, and the things they think are nothing but superficial-ities and foolishness. Whether I like it or not, I have to get along with them, and I don't always even realize that I'm conforming to them. It's dreadful! I could become one of them! It's terrible to see the world through their myopic eyes!"

The editor spoke with increasing excitement, and it seemed to the actress that in his words she heard the eternal protest of youth. This captivated her, this took her fancy, and she said: "You mustn't conform! You mustn't!"

"I mustn't," the young man agreed. "The doctor opened my eyes yesterday. At all costs I must get outside the vicious circle of this milieu. The vicious circle of this pettiness, of this mediocrity. I must leave," said the young man, "I must leave," he repeated.

"We talked about the fact," explained Havel to his wife, "that the ordinary taste of a small town creates a false ideal of beauty, which is essentially unerotic, even antierotic. Whereas genuine, explosive erotic magic remains unnoticed by those with such taste. There are women all around us who would be capable of leading a man to the most dizzying heights of sensual adventure, and no one here sees them."

"That's right," confirmed the young man.

"No one sees them," the doctor went on, "because they don't correspond to the local norms; that is to say, erotic magic shows itself by oddness rather than regularity, expressiveness rather than restraint, irregularity rather than ordinary prettiness."

"Yes," agreed the young man.

"You know Frantiska," said Havel to his wife.

"Yes," said the actress.

"And surely you know how many of my friends would give all their worldly goods for one night with her. I'd bet my life that in this town no one even notices her. Tell me, my dear editor, you know her, have you ever noticed that Frantiska is an extraordinary woman?"

"No, actually I haven't!" said the young man. "It never occurred to me to look at her as a woman!"

"Of course," said Havel. "You found her neither thin nor garrulous enough. She didn't have enough freckles!"

"Yes," said the young man unhappily. "Yesterday you found out what an idiot I am."

"But have you ever noticed how she walks?" continued Havel. "Have you ever noticed that her legs literally speak when she walks? My dear editor, if you heard what her legs were saying, you would blush, even though I know you're a hell of a libertine."

9

"You're making fools of innocent people," said the actress to her husband, when they had taken leave of the editor.

"You know very well that in me that's a sign of good humor. And I swear to you that this is the first time I've been in a good mood since I arrived here."

This time Dr. Havel was not lying; that morning when he had seen the bus coming into the terminal and caught sight of his wife behind the glass, and then seen her smiling on the step, he had been happy. And because the preceding days had stored up in him reserves of untouched gaiety, throughout the whole day he displayed a delight that was a bit mad. They strolled together through the colonnade, nibbled on sweet, round wafers, looked in on Frantiska and heard fresh information about her son's latest statements, completed the walk with the editor described in the preceding section, and made fun of the patients, who were walking through the streets for their health's sake. Upon this occasion, Dr. Havel noticed that several of the people who were walking about were staring at the actress; when he turned around he discovered that they were standing and looking back at them.

"You've been recognized," said Havel. "The people here have nothing to do, and they've become passionate moviegoers."

"Does it bother you?" asked the actress, who considered the publicity aspects of her profession a sin, for like all true lovers she longed for a love that was peaceful and hidden.

"On the contrary," said Havel, and he laughed. Then for a long time he amused himself with the childish game of trying to guess who, out of those people walking around, would recognize her and who would not, and he made bets with her as to how many people would recognize her on the next street. And old men, peasant women, children did turn around, but so also did the few good-looking women who were to be found at the spa at that time.

Havel, who in recent days had been experiencing humiliating invisibility, was pleasantly gratified by the attention of the passersby, and longed for the sparks of interest to alight, as much as possible, on him also; to this end, he put his arm around the actress's waist, bent down toward her, and whispered into her ear the most varied mixture of sweet-talk and lasciviousness, so that she too pressed herself against him in return and raised her merry eyes to his face. And Havel, beneath the many glances, felt how once more that he was regaining his lost visibility, that his dim features were becoming perceptible and conspicuous, and again he felt proud joy emanating from his body, from his gait, from his being.

While they were dawdling on the main street in front of the window displays, entwined in loverlike fashion, Havel caught sight of the blonde masseuse who had treated him so impolitely yesterday; she was standing in an empty hunting goods store, gabbing with the salesgirl. "Come," he said to his startled wife, "you are the best creature in the whole world; I want to give you a present," and he took her by the hand and led her into the store.

Both the chattering women fell silent; the masseuse took a long look at the actress, then a brief one at Havel, another look at the actress, and again one at Havel. Havel noted this with satisfaction but, without directing a single glance toward her, quickly scrutinized the goods on display; he saw antlers, haversacks, rifles, binoculars, walking sticks, muzzles for dogs.

"What would you like to see?" the salesgirl asked him.

"Just a minute," said Havel; finally he caught sight of some whistles under the glass of the counter and pointed to one of them. The salesgirl handed it to him, Havel put the whistle to his lips, whistled, then inspected it from all sides and once again whistled softly. "Excellent," he said to the salesgirl, and he placed before her the required five crowns. He gave the whistle to his wife.

The actress saw in this gift one of those childishnesses she loved in her husband, his clowning, his sense of non-sense, and she thanked him with a beautiful, amorous look. But that wasn't enough for Havel; he whispered to her: "Is that all your thanks for such a lovely present?" And so the actress kissed him. Neither woman took her eyes off them, even after they had left the store.

They resumed their walk in the streets and in the park, they nibbled on wafers, whistled on the whistle, sat on a bench, and made bets as to how many passersby would turn around to look at them. When in the evening they went into a restaurant, they nearly bumped into the woman who resembled a horse. She looked at them in surprise, stared at the actress for a long time, glanced briefly at Havel, then once again at the actress and, when she looked at Havel once more, involuntarily nodded to him. Havel nodded too, and bending toward his wife's ear, in a low voice asked if she loved him. The actress looked at him amorously and stroked his face.

Then they sat down at a table, ate lightly (for the actress took scrupulous care of her husband's diet), drank red wine (for Havel was allowed to drink only that), and a wave of emotion swept over Mrs. Havel. She leaned toward her husband, took him by the hand, and told him that this was one of the nicest days she had ever spent; she opened her heart to him, saying how unhappy she had been when he had left for the spa; once again she apologized for her jealous woman's letter and she thanked him for phoning her and asking her to join him here; she told him that it would have been worthwhile for her to come see him even for only a minute; then she talked at length about how life with him was a life of continuous torment and uncertainty, as if Havel were always on the verge of escaping her, but that just for this reason every day was a new experience for her, a new falling in love, a new gift.

Then they went off together to Havel's room, and the actress's joy soon reached its height.

10

Two days later Havel went again to his hydrotherapy session and again arrived somewhat late, because, to tell the truth, he was never on time anywhere. And there again was the blonde masseuse, only this time she didn't scowl at him, on the contrary, she smiled and addressed him as "Doctor," so Havel knew that she'd looked up his file, or else had inquired about him. Dr. Havel noted this interest with satisfaction and began to undress behind the screen in the cubicle. When the masseuse called to him that the bath was full, he self-assuredly stepped forward with his paunch thrust out and, with relish, sprawled in the water.

The masseuse turned on a faucet and asked him whether his wife was still at the spa. Havel said that she wasn't, and the masseuse asked if his wife would be acting again in some nice film. Havel said that she would, and the masseuse lifted up his right leg. When the stream of water tickled his sole the masseuse smiled and said that the doctor, as was evident, had a very sensitive body. Then they went on talking, and Havel mentioned that it was boring at the spa. The masseuse smiled very meaningfully and said that the doctor certainly knew how to arrange his life so as not to be bored. And when she was bending down low over him, running the nozzle of the hose over his chest, Havel praised her breasts, whose upper halves he could easily see from where he was lying, and the masseuse replied that the doctor had certainly seen more beautiful ones.

From all this it seemed quite obvious to Havel that his wife's brief visit had thoroughly transformed him in the eyes of this pleasant, muscular girl, that he had all of a sudden acquired charm and appeal, and, what is more, that his body was for her undoubtedly an opportunity that could secretly put her on intimate terms with a famous actress, make her equal to a celebrated woman everybody turned around to look at; Havel understood that suddenly everything was permitted him, everything was tacitly promised him in advance.

But then what often happens happened! When a man is contented, he gladly turns down an opportunity that presents itself, so as to be reassured about his blissful satiety. It was enough for Havel that the blonde woman had lost her insulting haughtiness, that she had a sweet voice and meek eyes, for the doctor no longer to desire her.

Then he had to turn over on his stomach, thrust his chin up out of the water, and let a stinging stream run over him from his heels to the nape of his neck. This position seemed to him to be a ritual position of humility and thanksgiving: He thought about his wife, about how beautiful she was, about how he loved her and she loved him, and also about how she was his lucky star that brought him the favors of chance and of muscular girls.

And when the massage was over and he stood up to step out of the bath, the masseuse, wet with perspiration, seemed to him so wholesomely and succulently pretty and her eyes so submissively affectionate that he longed to make an obeisance in the direction where, far away, he supposed his wife to be. It appeared to him that the masseuse's body was standing in the actress's large hand and that this hand was offering it to him like a message of love, like a gift. And it suddenly struck him as rudeness to his own wife to refuse this gift, to refuse this tender consideration. Therefore he smiled at the perspiring girl and said to her that he had freed himself this evening for her and would be waiting for her at seven o'clock at the hot springs. The girl consented, and Dr. Havel wrapped himself up in a large towel.

When he had dressed and combed his hair, he discovered that he was in an extraordinarily good mood. He felt like chatting, and for this reason stopped at Frantiska's. His visit suited her, for she too was in excellent spirits. She talked about all sorts of things, but always returned to the subject they had touched on at their last meeting: her age; in ambiguous sentences, she implied that a person should not give in to age, that a person's age is not always a disadvantage, and that it is an absolutly marvelous feeling when a person finds out that he or she can quietly talk as an equal with younger people. "And children aren't everything either," she said all at once for no reason. "You know that I love my children, but there are other things in life."

Frantiska's reflections did not depart even for an instant from their vague abstractness, and they would have unmistakably appeared to be mere idle talk to an uninitiated person. Only Havel was not an uninitiated person, and he discerned the purport hidden behind this idle talk. He gathered that his own happiness was only a link in a whole chain of happiness, and because he had a generous heart, he felt doubly good.

11

Yes, Dr. Havel had guessed correctly: the editor had dropped in on the woman doctor the very same day that his master had praised her. After just a few sentences he discovered within himself a surprising boldness, and he told her that he found her attractive and that he wanted to go out with her. The woman doctor stammered in alarm that she was older than he and that she had children. At this the editor gained self-confidence, and his words simply poured out: he claimed that she possessed a hidden beauty that was worth more than banal shapeliness; he praised her walk and told her that when she walked her legs were most expressive.

And two days after this declaration, at the same time that Dr. Havel was contentedly arriving at the hot springs, where already, from a distance, he could see the muscular blonde, the editor was impatiently pacing up and down in his narrow attic; he was almost certain of success, but this made him all the more fearful of some error or mishap that could deprive him of it; every little while he would open the door and look down the stairs. At last he caught sight of her.

The care with which Frantiska was dressed and made up changed her somewhat from the everyday woman who wore white pants and a white smock. To the excited young man it seemed that her erotic magic, heretofore only suspected, was now standing before him almost brazenly exposed, so that respectful diffidence assailed him. To overcome it he embraced the woman doctor in the doorway and began to kiss her frantically. She was alarmed by this sudden assault and begged him to let her sit down. He did let her, but he immediately sat at her feet and, on his knees, kissed her stockings. She put her hand in his hair and attempted to push him gently away.

Let us note what she said to him. First she repeated several times: "You must behave yourself, you must behave yourself; promise me that you'll behave yourself." When the young man said: "Yes, yes, I'll behave myself," and at the same time moved his mouth farther up the rough nylon, she said: "No, no, not that, not that"; and when he moved it still higher, she suddenly began to use his first name and declared: "You're a young devil, oh you're a young devil!"

Everything was decided by this declaration. The young man no longer encountered any resistance. He was carried away; he was carried away by himself, he was carried away by the swiftness of his success, he was carried away by Dr. Havel, whose genius had entered into him and now dwelled within him, he was carried away by the nakedness of the woman who was lying beneath him in amorous union. He longed to be a master, he longed to be a virtuoso, he longed to demonstrate his sensuality and savagery. He raised himself slightly above the woman doctor, with a passionate eye he examined her body lying there, and he murmured: "You're beautiful, you're magnificent, you're magnificent. . . ."

The doctor hid her belly with both hands and said: "You mustn't make fun of me—"

"What are you talking about? I'm not making fun of you! You're magnificent!"

"Don't look at me," she said, clasping him to her body so that he wouldn't see her. "I've had two children, you know."

"Two children?" said the young man uncomprehendingly.

"It shows. I don't want you to look at me."

This slowed the young man down a bit in his initial flight, and it was only with difficulty that he once again attained the proper arousal; in order to manage this better, he tried hard to reinforce with words his diminishing intoxication, and he whispered into the doctor's ear how beautiful it was that she was here with him naked, absolutely naked.

"You're sweet, you're terribly sweet," said the woman doctor.

The young man went on repeating the words about

her nakedness, and, he asked her whether it was also arousing for her that she was here with him naked.

"You're a child," said the woman doctor. "Of course it arouses me." But after a brief silence she added that so many doctors had already seen her naked that it had become ordinary. "More doctors than lovers," she said, and without interrupting their amorous movements she launched into an account of her difficulties in child-birth. "But it was worth it," she ended by saying: "I have two beautiful children. Beautiful, beautiful!"

Once again his arousal, come by with difficulty, was slipping away from the editor. He even had the impres-sion that they weren't making love but sitting in a café and chatting over a cup of tea. This outraged him. He began to make violent love to her again, and endeav-ored to engage her in more sensual thoughts: "When I came to see you last time, did you know that we would make love?"

"Did you?"

"I *wanted* to," said the editor, "I *wanted* to terribly!" and into the word "wanted" he put immense passion.

"You're like my son," the woman doctor said in his ear. "That kid wants everything too. I always ask him: 'Is it the moon you want?'"

That is how they made love: Frantiska talked to her heart's content.

Then when they were sitting next to each other on the couch, naked and tired, the woman doctor stroked the editor's hair and said: "You have a cute little mop like him."

"Like who?"

"My son."

"You're always thinking about your son," said the editor with timid disapproval.

"You know," she said proudly. "He's his mother's pet, he's his mother's pet."

Then she got up and dressed. And all of a sudden the feeling came over her in this young man's little room that she was young, that she was a really young woman, and she felt deliciously good. As she left she embraced the editor, and her eyes were moist with gratitude.

12

After a beautiful night, a beautiful day began for Dr. Havel. At breakfast he exchanged a few promising words with the woman who resembled a riding horse, and at ten o'clock, when he returned from his treatment, a loving letter from his wife awaited him in his room. Then he went to take a walk through the colonnade among the crowd of patients. He held the porcelain mug to his lips and he beamed with good humor. Women who at one time had passed by him without any show of interest now fastened their eyes on him, so that he nodded slightly to them in greeting. When he caught sight of the editor, he beckoned cheerfully to him: "I visited Frantiska this morning, and according to certain signs that cannot escape a good psychologist, it seems to me that you've met with success!"

The young man wanted nothing more than to confide in his master, but the events of the past evening had somewhat perflexed him. He wasn't sure if it had really been as great as it should have been, and that being so, he didn't know whether a precise and truthful account would raise or lower him in Havel's estimation. He was hesitant about what he should confide and what he shouldn't.

But when he now saw Havel's face beaming with cheer and shamelessness, he could do nothing but answer in a similarly cheerful and shameless tone, and, with enthusiastic words, he praised the woman Havel had recommended to him. He related how attractive he had found her when he had looked at her for the first time with eyes devoid of small-town prejudice, how she had quickly agreed to come to his place, and with what remarkable speed she had given herself to him.

When Dr. Havel put various precise and detailed questions to him, so as to analyze all of the matter's nuances, the young man willy-nilly came closer and closer to the truth, finally acknowledging that although he had been perfectly satisfied with everything, the woman doctor's conversation while making love had put him out somewhat.

Dr. Havel found this very interesting, and, having persuaded the editor to repeat the dialogue to him in detail, he interrupted the account with enthusiastic exclamations: "That's excellent! Perfect!" "Oh, that eternal mother's heart!" And: "My friend, I really envy you!"

At that moment the woman who resembled a riding horse stopped in front of the two men. Dr. Havel bowed, and the woman offered him her hand: "Don't be angry," she apologized, "I'm a tiny bit late."

"Never mind," said Havel. "I've been enjoying myself enormously with my friend here. You must forgive me if I finish my conversation with him."

And, not letting go of the tall woman's hand, he turned to the editor: "My dear friend, what you've told me surpasses all my expectations. You must understand that the pleasures of the body left only to its silence are tiresomely similar. In this silence one woman becomes like another and all of them are forgotten in all the others. And surely we throw ourselves into erotic pleasures above all in order to remember them. So that their luminous points will connect our youth with our old age by means of a shining ribbon! So that they will preserve our memory in an eternal flame! And take it from me, my friend, only a word uttered at this most ordinary of moments is capable of illuminating it in such a way that it remains unforgettable. They say of me that I'm a collector of women. In reality I'm far more a collector of words. Believe me, you'll never forget yesterday evening, and you'll be happy about that all your life!"

Then he nodded to the young man, and still holding the tall woman who resembled a horse by the hand, he moved away slowly with her along the colonnade.

Eduard and God

1

Let me begin Eduard's story in his older brother's little house in the country. His brother was lying on the couch and saying to Eduard: "Ask the old hag. Never mind, just go and talk to her. Of course she's a pig, but I believe that even in such creatures a conscience exists. Just because she once did me dirt, now maybe she'll be glad if you'll let her make up for her past misdeed."

Eduard's brother was always the same: a good-natured guy and a lazy one. He probably had been lolling on the couch this way in his student attic when, quite a few years ago (Eduard was still a little boy then), he had lazed and snored away the day of Stalin's death. The next day, still unaware of the news, he had turned up at the university and caught sight of his fellow student, Comrade Cechackova, standing in ostentatious rigidity in the middle of the hall like a statue of grief. Three times he circled her and then began to roar with laughter. The offended girl denounced her fellow student's laughter as political provocation, and Eduard's brother had to abandon his studies and go to work in a village, where since that time he had acquired a house, a dog, a wife, two children, and even a weekend cottage.

243

In this village house, then, he was now lying on the couch and explaining to Eduard: "We used to call her the chastising working-class whip. But that shouldn't intimidate you. Nowadays she's an aging woman, and she always had a weakness for young men, so she'll be helpful."

Eduard was at that time very young. He had just graduated from teachers college (the course from which his brother had been expelled) and was looking for a position. The next day, following his brother's advice, he knocked on the directress's office door. She was a tall, bony woman with greasy black hair, black eyes, and black fuzz under her nose. Her ugliness relieved him of the shyness to which feminine beauty still always reduced him, so that he managed to talk to her in a relaxed manner, amiably, even courteously. The directress was evidently delighted by his approach, and several times she said with perceptible elation: "We need young people here." She promised to find a place for him.

2

And so Eduard became a teacher in a small Bohemian town. This made him neither happy nor sad. He always tried hard to distinguish between the serious and the unserious, and he put his teaching career into the category of *unserious*. Not that teaching itself was unserious (in fact he was deeply attached to it, because he knew that he would not be able to earn a living any other way), but he considered it unserious in terms of his true nature. He hadn't chosen it. Society's requirements, his party record, his high school diploma, and his entrance examinations had imposed it on him. The interlocking conjunction of all these forces eventually dumped him (as a crane drops a sack onto a truck) from high school into teachers college. He didn't want to go there (his brother's failure was a bad omen), but eventually he acquiesced. He understood, however, that his occupation would be among the fortuitous aspects of his life. It would be attached to him like a false mustache, which is something laughable.

But if what is *obligatory* is unserious (laughable), what is serious is probably *optional*: in his new abode Eduard soon found a girl who struck him as beautiful, and he began to pursue her with a seriousness that was almost sincere. Her name was Alice and she was, as he discovered to his great sorrow on their first dates, very reserved and virtuous.

Many times during their evening walks he had tried to put his arm around her so that he could touch the region of her right breast from behind, and each time she had seized his hand and pushed it away. One evening when he was trying this once again and she (once again) was pushing his hand away, she stopped and asked: "Do you believe in God?"

With his sensitive ears Eduard caught a discreet insistence in this question, and he immediately forgot about the breast.

"Do you?" Alice repeated her question, and Eduard didn't dare answer. Let us not condemn him for fearing to be frank; as a newcomer in this town he felt lonely, and he was too attracted to Alice to risk losing her favor over a single simple answer.

"And you?" he asked in order to gain time.

"Yes, I do." And once again she urged him to answer her.

Until this time it had never occurred to him to believe in God. He understood, however, that he must not admit this. On the contrary, he saw that he should take advantage of the opportunity and knock together from faith in God a nice Trojan horse, within whose belly, according to the ancient example, he would slip into the girl's heart unobserved. Only it wasn't so easy for Eduard simply to say to Alice, "I believe in God"; he wasn't at all impudent, and he was ashamed to lie; the simplicity of lying repelled him; if a lie was absolutely necessary, he wanted it to remain as close as possible to the truth. For that reason he replied in an exceptionally thoughtful voice:

"I don't really know, Alice, what I should say to you about this. Certainly I believe in God. But . . ." He paused and Alice glanced up at him in surprise. "But I want to be completely frank with you. May I?"

"You must be frank," she said. "Otherwise surely there wouldn't be any sense in our being together."

"Really?"

"Really," said Alice.

"Sometimes I'm troubled by doubts," said Eduard in a choked voice. "Sometimes I wonder whether he really exists."

"But how can you doubt that?" Alice nearly shouted.

Eduard was silent, and after a moment's reflection a familiar thought struck him: "When I see so much evil around me, I often wonder how it is possible that a God exists who would permit all that."

That sounded so sad that Alice seized his hand: "Yes, the world is indeed full of evil. I know this only too well. But for that reason you must believe in God. Without him all this suffering would be in vain. Nothing would have any meaning. And if that were so, I couldn't live at all."

"Perhaps you're right," said Eduard thoughtfully, and on Sunday he went to church with her. He dipped his fingers in the font and crossed himself. Then there was the Mass and people sang, and with the others he sang a hymn whose tune was familiar, but to which he didn't know the words. Instead of the prescribed words he chose only various vowels, and he always hit each note a fraction of a second behind the others, because he only dimly recollected even the tune. Yet the moment he became certain of the note, he let his voice ring out fully, so that for the first time in his life he realized that he had a beautiful bass. Then they all began to recite the Lord's Prayer, and some old ladies knelt. He could not hold back a compelling desire to kneel too on the stone floor. He crossed himself with impressive arm movements and experienced the marvelous feeling of being able to do something that he had never done in his life, neither in the classroom nor on the street nor anywhere. He felt marvelously free.

When it was all over, Alice looked at him with a radiant expression in her eyes. "Can you still say that you doubt he exists?"

"No."

And Alice said: "I would like to teach you to love him just as I do."

They were standing on the broad steps of the church and Eduard's soul was full of laughter. Unfortunately, just at that moment the directress was walking by, and she saw them.

3

This was bad. We must recall (for those at risk of losing the historical background) that although it is true that people weren't forbidden to go to church, nonetheless churchgoing was not without a certain danger.

This is not so difficult to understand. Those who had fought for what they called the revolution maintained a great pride: the pride of being *on the correct side of the front lines*. Ten or twelve years later (around the time of our story) the front lines began to melt away, and with them the correct side. No wonder the former supporters of the revolution feel cheated and are quick to seek *substitute* fronts; thanks to religion they can (in their role as atheists struggling against believers) stand again on the correct side and retain their habitual and precious sense of their own superiority.

But to tell the truth, the substitute front was also useful to others, and it will perhaps not be too premature to disclose that Alice was one of them. Just as the directress wanted to be on the *correct* side, Alice wanted to be on the *opposite* side. During the revolution they had nationalized her papa's shop, and Alice hated those who had done this to him. But how should she show her hatred? Perhaps by taking a knife and avenging her father? But this sort of thing is not the custom in Bohemia. Alice had a better means for expressing her opposition: she began to believe in God.

Thus the Lord came to the aid of both sides, and, thanks to him, Eduard found himself between two fires.

When on Monday morning the directress came up to Eduard in the staff room, he felt very ill at ease. There was no way he could invoke the friendly atmosphere of their first interview, because since that time (whether through artlessness or carelessness), he had never again engaged in flirtatious conversation with her. The directress therefore had good reason to address him with a conspicuously cold smile: "We saw each other yesterday, didn't we?"

"Yes, we did," said Eduard.

The directress went on: "I can't understand how a young man can go to church." Eduard shrugged his shoulders uncomfortably, and the directress shook her head. "A young man like you."

"I went to see the baroque interior of the cathedral," said Eduard by way of an excuse.

"Ah, so that's it," said the directress ironically. "I didn't know you were interested in architecture."

This conversation was not at all pleasant for Eduard. He remembered that his brother had circled his fellow student three times and then roared with laughter. It seemed to him that family history was repeating itself, and he felt afraid. On Saturday he made his excuses over the telephone to Alice, saying that he wouldn't be going to church because he had a cold.

"You're a real sissy," Alice rebuked him when they saw each other again during the week, and it seemed to Eduard that her words sounded cold. So he began to tell her (enigmatically and vaguely, because he was ashamed to admit his fear and his real reasons) about the wrongs being done him at school, and about the horrible directress who was persecuting him without cause. He wanted to arouse her compassion, but Alice said: "My woman boss, on the contrary, isn't bad at all," and, giggling, she began to relate stories about her work. Eduard listened to her merry voice and became more and more gloomy.

4

Ladies and gentlemen, those were weeks of torment! Eduard longed hellishly for Alice. Her body fired him up, and yet this very body was utterly inaccessible to him. The settings in which their dates took place were also tormenting; either they wandered for an hour or two in the streets after dark or they went to the movies; the banality and the negligible erotic possibilities of these two variants (there weren't any others) prompted Eduard to think that perhaps he would achieve more success if they could meet in a different environment. Once, with an ingenuous face, he proposed that for the weekend they go to the country and visit his brother, who had a cottage in a wooded valley by a river. He excitedly described the innocent beauties of nature, but Alice (naive and credulous in every other respect) swiftly saw through him and categorically refused. It wasn't Alice alone who was resisting him. It was Alice's (eternally vigilant and wary) God himself.

This God embodied a single idea (he had no other wishes or concerns): he forbade extramarital sex. He was therefore a rather comical God, but let's not laugh at Alice for that. Of the Ten Commandments Moses gave to the people, fully nine didn't endanger her soul at all; she didn't feel like killing or not honoring her father, or coveting her neighbor's wife; only one commandment she felt to be not self-evident and therefore posed a genuine challenge: the famous seventh, which forbids fornication. In order to practice, show, and prove her religious faith, she had to devote her entire attention to this single commandment. And so out of a vague, diffuse, and abstract God, she created a God who was specific, comprehensible, and concrete: God Antifornicator.

I ask you where in fact does fornication begin? Every woman fixes this boundary for herself according to totally mysterious criteria. Alice quite happily allowed Eduard to kiss her, and after many, many attempts she eventually became reconciled to letting him stroke her breasts. However, at the middle of her body, let's say at her navel, she drew a strict and uncompromising line, below which lay the area of sacred prohibitions, the area of Moses's denial and the anger of the Lord.

Eduard began to read the Bible and to study basic theological literature. He had decided to fight Alice with her own weapons.

"Alice dear," he then said to her, "if we love God, nothing is forbidden. If we long for something, it's because of his will. Christ wanted nothing but that we should all be ruled by love."

"Yes," said Alice, "but a different love from the one you're thinking of."

"There's only one love," said Eduard.

"That would certainly suit you," she said, "Only God set down certain commandments, and we must abide by them."

"Yes, the Old Testament God," said Eduard, "but not the Christian God."

"How's that? Surely there's only one God," objected Alice.

"Yes," said Eduard, "only the Jews of the Old Testament understood him a little differently from the way we do. Before the coming of Christ, men had to abide above all by a specific system of God's commandments and laws. What went on in a man's soul was not so important. But Christ considered some of these prohibitions and regulations to be something external. For him the most important thing was what a man was like deep down. When a man is true to his own ardent, believing heart, everything he does is good and pleasing to God. That's why St. Paul said: 'Everything is pure to the man who is pure at heart.'"

"But I wonder if you are pure at heart."

"And Saint Augustine," continued Eduard, "said: 'Love God and do what it pleases you to do.' Do you understand, Alice? Love God, and do what it pleases you to do."

"But what pleases you will never please me," she replied, and Eduard understood that his theological assault had foundered completely; therefore he said:

"You don't love me."

"I do," said Alice in a terribly matter-of-fact way. "And that's why I don't want us to do anything we shouldn't do."

As I have already mentioned, these were weeks of torment. And the torment was that much greater because Eduard's desire for Alice was not only the desire of a body for a body; on the contrary, the more she refused

Laughable Loves

him her body, the more lonesome and afflicted he
became and the more he coveted her heart as well. However, neither her body nor her heart wanted to do anything about it; they were equally cold, equally wrapped
up in themselves and self-satisfied.

It was precisely this unruffled moderation of hers
that exasperated Eduard most. Although in other
respects he was quite a sober young man, he began to
long for some extreme action through which he could
drive Alice out of her unruffled state. And because it
was too risky to provoke her through blasphemy or
cynicism (to which by nature he was attracted), he had
to go to the opposite (and therefore far more difficult)
extreme, which would coincide with Alice's own position but would be so overdone as to put her to shame.
In other words Eduard began to exaggerate his reli-
giousness. He didn't miss a single visit to church (his
desire for Alice was greater than his fear of boredom),
and once there he behaved with eccentric humility: he
knelt at every opportunity, while Alice prayed beside
him and crossed herself standing, because she was
afraid to get a run in her stockings.

One day he criticized her for her lukewarm religiosity.
He reminded her of Jesus' words: "Not everyone who
says to me 'Lord, Lord' shall enter the kingdom of
heaven." He criticized her, saying that her faith was for-
mal, external, shallow. He criticized her for being too
pleased with herself. He criticized her for being unaware
of anyone but herself.

As he was saying all this (Alice was not prepared for his

attack and defended herself feebly), he suddenly caught sight of an old, roadwide cross with a rusty Christ on it. He briskly withdrew his arm from Alice's, stopped (as a protest against the girl's indifference and as a sign of his new offensive), and crossed himself ostentatiously. But he did not really to see how this affected Alice, because at that moment he spied on the other side of the street the woman janitor of the school. She was looking at him. Eduard realized that he was lost.

5

His fears were confirmed when two days later the woman janitor stopped him in the corridor and loudly informed him that he was to present himself the next day at twelve o'clock at the directress's office: "We have something to talk to you about, comrade."

Eduard was overcome by anxiety. In the evening he met Alice so that, as usual, they could stroll in the streets for an hour or two, but Eduard had abandoned his religious fervor. He was downcast and longed to confide to Alice what had happened to him, but he didn't dare, because he knew that in order to save his unloved (but indispensable) job, he was ready to betray the good Lord without hesitation. For this reason he preferred not to say a word about the inauspicious summons, so he couldn't even get any consolation. The following day he entered the directress's office in a mood of utter dejection.

In the room four judges awaited him: the directress, the woman janitor, one of Eduard's colleagues (a tiny man with glasses), and an unknown (gray-haired) gentleman, whom the others called "Comrade Inspector." The directress asked Eduard to be seated, and told him they had invited him for just a friendly and unofficial talk. For, she said, the manner in which Eduard had been conducting himself in his life outside the school was making them all uneasy. As she said this she looked at the inspector, who nodded his head in agreement, then at the bespectacled teacher, who had been watching her attentively the whole time and who now, intercepting her glance, launched into a long speech. He said that we wanted to educate healthy young people without prejudices and that we had complete responsibility for them because we (the teachers) served as models for them. Precisely for this reason, he said, we could not countenance a religious person within our walls. He developed this idea at length and finally declared that Eduard's behavior was a disgrace to the whole school.

A few minutes earlier Eduard had been convinced that he would deny his recently acquired God and admit that his church attendance and his crossing himself in public were only jokes. Now, however, faced with the situation, he felt that it was impossible to tell the truth. He could not, after all, say to these four people, so serious and so passionate, that they were impassioned about a misunderstanding, a bit of foolishness. He understood that to do that would be involuntarily to mock their seriousness, and he also realized that what they were expecting from him were only quibbles and excuses, which they were prepared in advance to reject. He understood (in a flash, there wasn't time for lengthy reflection) that at that moment the most important thing was for him to appear truthful or, more precisely, that his statements should resemble the idea of him they had constructed; if he wanted, to a degree, to correct that idea, he also, to a degree, had to accept it.

"Comrades, may I be frank?"

"Of course," said the directress. "After all, that's why you're here."

"And you won't be angry?"

"Say what you have to say," said the directress.

"Very well, I'm going to confess to you then. I really do believe in God."

He glanced at his judges, and it seemed to him that they all exhaled with satisfaction. Only the woman janitor snapped at him. "In this day and age, comrade? In this day and age?"

Eduard went on: "I knew that you'd be angry if I told the truth. But I don't know how to lie. Don't ask me to lie to you."

The directress said (gently): "No one wants you to lie. It's good that you are telling the truth. But please tell me how you, a young man, can believe in God!"

"These days, when we send rockets to the moon!" The teacher lost his temper.

"I can't help it," said Eduard. "I don't want to believe in God. Really I don't."

"How can you say you don't want to believe, if you do?" The gray-haired gentleman (in an exceedingly kind tone of voice) joined the conversation.

"I don't want to believe, but I do believe." Eduard quietly repeated his confession.

The bespectacled teacher laughed. "But there's a contradiction in that!"

"Comrades, I'm telling it the way it is," said Eduard. "I know very well that faith in God leads us away from reality. What would socialism come to if everyone believed that the world is in God's hands? No one would do anything and everyone would just rely on God."

"Exactly," agreed the directress.

"No one has ever yet proved that God exists," stated the teacher.

Eduard continued: "The difference between the history of mankind and prehistory is that man has taken his fate into his own hands and no longer needs God."

"Faith in God leads to fatalism," said the directress.

"Faith in God belongs to the Middle Ages," said Eduard, and then the directress said something again and the teacher said something and Eduard said something and the inspector said something, and they were all in complete accord, until finally the teacher with glasses exploded, interrupting Eduard: "So why do you cross yourself in the street, when you know all this?"

Eduard looked at him with an immensely sad

expression and then said: "Because I believe in God."

"But there's a contradiction in that!" repeated the teacher joyfully.

"Yes," admitted Eduard, "there is a contradiction between knowledge and faith. I recognize that faith in God leads to obscurantism. I recognize that it would be better if God didn't exist. But what can I do when here, deep down"—at this he pointed to his heart—"I feel that he does exist? You see, comrades, I'm telling it to you the way it is! It's better that I confess to you, because I don't want to be a hypocrite. I want you to know what I'm really like," and he hung his head.

The teacher had a shortsighted view; he didn't know that even the strictest revolutionary considers violence merely a necessary evil and believes that the intrinsic *good* of the revolution lies in reeducation. He, who had become a revolutionary overnight, did not enjoy much respect from the directress, and he did not suspect that at this moment Eduard, who had placed himself at his judges' disposal as a difficult case and yet as an object capable of being reeducated, had a thousand times more value than he. And because he didn't suspect it, he attacked Eduard with severity and declared that people who did not know how to part with their medieval faith belonged in the Middle Ages and should leave their position in a present-day school.

The directress let him finish his speech, then administered her rebuke: "I don't like it when heads roll. This comrade has been sincere, and he told us the truth. We must know how to respect that." Then she turned to

Eduard. "The comrades are right, of course, when they say that religious people cannot educate our youth. What do you yourself suggest?"

"I don't know, comrades," said Eduard unhappily.

"This is what I think," said the inspector. "The struggle between the old and the new goes on not only between classes, but also within each individual. Just such a struggle is going on inside our comrade here. With his reason he knows, but his feelings pull him back. We must help our comrade in this struggle, so that reason may triumph."

The directress nodded. Then she said: "I myself will take charge of him."

6

Eduard had thus averted the most pressing danger: his fate as a teacher was now in the hands of the directress exclusively, which was entirely to his satisfaction: he remembered his brother's observation that the directress had a weakness for young men, and with all his vacillating youthful self-confidence (now deflated, then exaggerated) he resolved to win the contest by gaining as a man his sovereign's favor.

When, as agreed, he visited her a few days later in her office, he tried to assume a light tone and used every opportunity to slip an intimate remark or bit of subtle flattery into the conversation, or to emphasize with discreet ambiguity his singular position as a man at a woman's mercy. But he was not to be permitted to choose the tone of the conversation. The directress spoke to him affably, but with the utmost restraint; she asked him what he was reading, then she herself named some books and recommended that he read them; she evidently wanted to embark on the lengthy job to be done on his thinking. Their short meeting ended with her inviting him to her place.

As a result of the directress's reserve, Eduard's self-confidence was deflated again, so he entered her studio apartment meekly, with no intention of impressing her with his masculine charm. She seated him in an arm-chair and, in a friendly tone, asked him what he felt like having: some coffee, perhaps? He said no. Some alcohol then? He was embarrassed: "If you have some cognac . . ." and was immediately afraid that he had been presumptuous. But the directress replied affably: "No, I don't have cognac, but I do have a little wine," and she brought over a half-empty bottle, whose contents were just sufficient to fill two glasses.

Then she told Eduard that he must not regard her as an inquisitor; after all, everyone has a complete right to convictions he believes to be correct. Naturally, one can of course (she added at once) wonder whether such a person is fit to be a teacher; for that reason, she said, they had had to summon Eduard (although they hadn't been happy about it) and have a talk with him, and they (at least she and the inspector) were very pleased with the frank manner in which he had spoken to them, and the fact that he had not denied anything. Then she said that she had talked with the inspector about Eduard for a very long time, and they had decided that they would summon him for another interview in six months' time and that until then the directress would help his development through her influence. And once again she emphasized that she merely wanted give him *friendly help*, that she was neither an inquisitor nor a cop. Then she mentioned the teacher who had attacked Eduard so sharply, and she said: "That man is hiding something himself, and so he would be glad to sacrifice others. Also, the woman janitor is letting it be known everywhere that you are insolent and pigheadedly stick to your opinions, as she puts it. She can't be talked out of her view that you should be dismissed from the school. Of course I don't agree with her, but on the other hand you must understand her. It wouldn't please me either if someone who crosses himself publicly in the street were teaching my children."

Thus the directress showed Eduard in a single outpouring of sentences, how attractive were the prospects of her clemency and also how menacing the prospects of her severity. And then to prove that their meeting was genuinely a friendly one, she digressed to other subjects: She talked about books, showed Eduard her library, and asked how he liked the school, and after his conventional reply, she herself spoke at length. She said that she was grateful to destiny for her position; that she liked her work because it was a means for her to educate children and thus be in continuous and real touch with the future, and that only the future could, in the end, justify all this suffering, of which she said ("Yes, we must admit it") there was plenty. "If I did not believe that I am living for something more than just my own life, I probably couldn't live at all."

These words suddenly sounded very sincere, and it was not clear to Eduard whether the directress was trying to confess or to commence the expected ideological polemic about the meaning of life. Eduard decided to interpret them in their personal sense, and he asked her in a choked, discreet voice:

"And what about your own life?"

"My life?"

"Yes, your own life. Doesn't it satisfy you?"

A bitter smile appeared on her face, and Eduard felt almost sorry for her at that moment. She was pitifully ugly: her black hair cast a shadow over her bony, elongated face, and the black fuzz under her nose began to look as conspicuous as a mustache. Suddenly he glimpsed all the sorrow of her life. He perceived the Gypsy-like features that revealed violent sensuality, and he perceived the ugliness that revealed the impossibility of appeasing that violence; he imagined her passionately turning into a living statue of grief upon Stalin's death, passionately sitting up late at thousands of meetings, passionately struggling against poor Jesus. And he understood that all this was merely a sad outlet for her desire, which could not flow where she wished it to. Eduard was young, and his inclination toward compassion had not yet vanished. He looked at the directress with understanding. She, however, as if ashamed of having involuntarily fallen silent, now assumed a brisk tone and went on: "That's not the question at all, Eduard. One doesn't live for oneself. One always lives for something." She looked deeply into his eyes: "But it's a matter of knowing for what. For something real or for something fictitious? God is a beautiful idea. But the future of man, Eduard, is a reality. And I have lived for reality; I have sacrificed everything for reality."

She spoke with such conviction, that Eduard did not stop feeling that sudden rush of understanding that had awakened in him a short while before; it struck him as stupid that he should be lying so brazenly to another human being, and it seemed to him that this intimate moment in their conversation offered him the opportunity to cast away finally his unworthy (and, moreover, difficult) deception.

"But I agree with you completely," he quickly assured her. "I too prefer reality. Don't take my piety so seriously!"

He soon learned that a man should never let himself be led astray by a rash fit of emotion. The directress looked at him in surprise and said with perceptible coldness: "Don't pretend. I liked you because you were frank. Now you're pretending to be something that you aren't."

No, Eduard was not to be permitted to step out of the

religious costume in which he had clothed himself. He quickly reconciled himself to this and tried hard to correct the bad impression: "No, I didn't mean to be evasive. Of course I believe in God, I would never deny that. I only wanted to say that I also believe in the future of humanity, in progress and all that. If I didn't believe in that, what would my work as a teacher be for, what would children be born for, and what would our lives be for? And I've come to think that it is also God's will that society continue to advance toward something better. I have thought that a man can believe in God and in communism, that the two can be reconciled."

"No," said the directress with maternal authoritativeness. "The two are irreconcilable."

"I know," said Eduard sadly. "Don't be angry with me."

"I'm not angry. You are still a young man and you obstinately stick to what you believe. No one understands you the way I do. After all I was young once too. I know what it's like to be young. And I like your youthfulness. Yes, I rather like you. . . ."

And now it finally happened. Neither earlier nor later, but now, at precisely the right moment. (That right moment, as can be seen, Eduard had not chosen; it was the moment itself that made use of Eduard to make it happen.) When the directress said she rather liked him he replied, not too expressively:

"I like you too."

"Really?"

"Really."

"Well, I never! I'm an old woman. . . ." objected the directress.

"That's not true," Eduard had to say.

"But it is," said the directress.

"You're not at all old, that's nonsense," he had to say very resolutely.

"Do you think so?"

"Of course. I like you very much."

"Don't lie. You know you shouldn't lie."

"I'm not lying. You're pretty."

"Pretty?" The directress made a face to show that she didn't really believe it.

"Yes, pretty," said Eduard, and because he was struck by the obvious improbability of his assertion, he at once took pains to support it: "I'm mad about dark-haired women like you."

"You like dark-haired women?" asked the directress.

"I'm mad about them," said Eduard.

"And why haven't you come by all the time that you've been at the school? I had the feeling that you were avoiding me."

"I was hesitating," said Eduard. "Everyone would have said I was sucking up to you. No one would have believed that I was coming to see you only because I liked you."

"But there's nothing to be afraid of now," said the directress. "Now it's been *decreed* that we must see each other from time to time."

She looked into his eyes with her large brown irises (let us admit that in themselves her eyes were beautiful), and just before he left she lightly stroked his hand, so that this foolish fellow went away feeling the elation of a winner.

7

Eduard was sure that the unpleasant matter had been settled to his advantage, and the next Sunday, feeling carefree and impudent, he went to church with Alice and not only that, he went there full of self-confidence, for (although this arouses in us a compassionate smile) his visit to the directress retrospectively provided him with glaring evidence of his masculine appeal.

In addition this particular Sunday in church he noticed that Alice was somewhat different: As soon as they met she took his arm and even in church clung to him; while formerly she had behaved modestly and inconspicuously, now she kept looking around and smilingly greeted at least ten acquaintances.

This was curious, and Eduard didn't understand it.

Then two days later, as they were walking together along the streets after dark, Eduard became aware to his amazement that her kisses, once so sadly matter-of-fact, had become damp, warm, and fervent. When they stopped for a moment under a streetlight, he found her eyes looking amorously at him.

"Let me tell you this: I love you," Alice blurted out, and immediately she covered his mouth. "No, no, don't say anything. I'm ashamed of myself. I don't want to hear anything."

Again they walked a little way, again they stopped, and Alice said: "Now I understand everything. I understand why you reproached me for being too comfortable in my faith."

Eduard, however, didn't understand anything; so he too didn't say anything; when they had walked a bit farther, Alice said: "And you didn't say anything to me. Why didn't you say anything to me?"

"And what should I have said to you?" asked Eduard.

"Yes, that's really you," she said with quiet enthusiasm. "Others would put on airs, but you're silent. But that's exactly why I love you."

Eduard began to understand what she was talking about, but nevertheless he asked: "What are you talking about?"

"About what happened to you."

"And who told you about it?"

"Come on! Everybody knows about it. They summoned you, they threatened you, and you laughed in their faces. You didn't renounce anything. Everyone admires you."

"But I didn't tell anyone about it."

"Don't be naive. A thing like that gets around. After all, it's no small matter. How often nowadays do you find someone with some courage?"

Eduard knew that in a small town every event is quickly turned into a legend, but he hadn't suspected that the worthless episodes he'd been involved in, whose significance he'd never overestimated, possessed the stuff of which legends are made; he hadn't sufficiently realized how very useful he was to his fellow citizens who, as is well known, adore martyrs, for such men soothingly reassure them about their sweet inactivity, and corroborate their view that life provides only one alternative: to obey or be destroyed. Nobody doubted that Eduard would be destroyed, and admiringly and complacently they all passed the news on, until now, through Alice, he himself encountered the splendid image of his own crucifixion. He reacted calmly and said: "But my not renouncing anything is completely natural. Anyone would else would do the same."

"Anyone?" Alice shouted. "Look around to see how people behave! How cowardly they are! They'd renounce their own mothers!"

Eduard was silent, and Alice was silent. They walked along holding hands. Then Alice said in a whisper: "I would do anything for you."

No one had ever said such words to Eduard; they were an unexpected gift. Of course Eduard knew that they were an undeserved gift, but he said to himself that if fate withheld from him deserved gifts, he had a complete right to accept these undeserved ones. Therefore he said: "No one can do anything for me anymore."

"How's that?" whispered Alice.

"They'll drive me from the school, and those who speak of me today as a hero won't lift a finger for me. Only one thing is certain. I'll remain entirely alone."

"You won't," said Alice, shaking her head.

"I will," said Eduard.

"You won't!" Alice almost shouted.

"They've all abandoned me."

"I'll never abandon you," said Alice.

"You'll end up abandoning me too," said Eduard sadly.

"Never," said Alice.

"No, Alice," said Eduard. "You don't love me. You've never loved me."

"That's not true," whispered Alice, and Eduard noticed with satisfaction that her eyes were wet.

"You don't, Alice. A person can feel that sort of thing. You were always extremely cold to me. A woman who loves a man doesn't behave like that. I know that very well. And now you feel compassion for me, because you know they want to destroy me. But you don't really love me, and I don't want you to deceive yourself about it."

They walked still farther, silently, holding hands. Alice cried quietly for a while, then all at once she stopped walking and amid sobs she said: "No, that's not true. You have no right to say that. That's not true."

"It is," said Eduard, and when Alice did not stop crying, he suggested that on Saturday they go to the country. In a pretty valley by the river was his brother's cottage, where they could be alone.

Alice's face was wet with tears as she dumbly nodded her assent.

8

That was on Tuesday, and when on Thursday he was again invited to the directress's studio apartment, he made his way there with cheerful self-assurance, for he had absolutely no doubt that his natural charm would definitively dissolve the church scandal into a little puff of smoke. But this is how life goes: a man imagines that he is playing his role in a particular play, and he does not suspect that in the meantime they have changed the scenery without his noticing, and he unknowingly finds himself in the middle of a rather different performance.

He was again seated in the armchair opposite the directress. Between them was a little table and on it a bottle of cognac and two glasses. And this bottle of cognac was precisely that new prop by which a perspicacious and sober man would immediately have recognized that the church scandal was no longer the matter in question.

But innocent Eduard was so infatuated with himself that at first he didn't realize this at all. He took part with good humor in the opening conversation (whose subject was vague and general), emptied the glass that was offered him, and was guilelessly bored. After half an hour or an hour the directress inconspicuously changed to more personal topics; she talked a lot about herself, and from her words there emerged before Eduard the image that she wanted: that of a sensible, middle-aged woman, not too happy, but reconciled to her lot in a dignified way, a woman who regretted nothing and even expressed satisfaction that she was not married, because only in this way could she fully enjoy her independence and privacy. This life had provided her with a pretty apartment, where she felt happy and where perhaps now Eduard was also not too uncomfortable.

"No, it's really very nice here," said Eduard, and he said it glumly, because just at that moment he had stopped feeling good. The bottle of cognac (which he had inadvertently asked for on his first visit and which was now hurried to the table with such menacing readiness), the four walls of the studio apartment (creating a space that was becoming ever more constricting and confining), the directress's monologue (focusing on subjects ever more personal), her gaze (dangerously fixed on him), all this caused *the change of program* to begin finally to get to him; he realized that he had entered into a situation whose development was irrevocably predetermined; he clearly realized that his livelihood was jeopardized not by the directress's aversion, but by just the contrary, his physical aversion to this skinny woman with the fuzz under her nose, who was urging him to drink. His anxiety made his throat tighten.

He obeyed the directress and emptied his glass, but now his anxiety was so strong that the alcohol had no effect on him. On the other hand after a couple of drinks the directress was already so thoroughly carried away that she abandoned her usual sobriety, and her words acquired an exaltation that was almost threatening: "One thing I envy you," she said, "is that you are so young. You can't know yet what disappointment is, what disillusion is. You still see the world as full of hope and beauty."

She leaned across the table in Eduard's direction and in gloomy silence (with a smile that was rigidly forced) fixed her frightfully large eyes on him, while he said to himself that if he didn't manage to get a bit drunk, he'd be in real trouble before the evening was over; to that end he poured some cognac into his glass and downed it quickly.

And the directress went on: "But I want to see it like that! The way you do!" And then she got up from the armchair, thrust out her chest, and said: "Is it true that you like me? Is it true?" And she walked around the little table and grabbed Eduard by the sleeve. "Is it true?"

"Yes," said Eduard.

"Come, let's dance," she said, and letting go of Eduard's hand she skipped over to the radio and turned the dial until she found some dance music. Then she stood over Eduard with a smile.

Eduard got up, seized the directress, and began to guide her around the room to the rhythm of the music. Every now and then the directress would tenderly lay her head on his shoulder, then suddenly raise it again, to gaze into his eyes, then, after another little while, she would softly sing along with the melody.

Eduard felt so ill at ease that several times he stopped dancing to have a drink. He longed for nothing more than to put an end to the horror of this inter-minable trudging around, but also he feared nothing more, for the horror of what would follow the dancing seemed to him even more unbearable. And so he con-tinued to guide the lady who was singing to herself around the room, and at the same time intently (and with anxious impatience) watching for the desired effect on him of the alcohol. When it finally seemed to him that his brain was sufficiently deadened by the cognac, with his right arm he firmly pressed the direc-tress against his body and put his left hand on her breast.

Yes, he did the very thing that had been frightening him the whole evening; he would have given anything not to have had to do this, but if he did it nevertheless, then believe me, it was only because he really *had to*: the situation he had got into at the very beginning of the evening offered no way out; though it was probably possible to slow its course, it was impossible to stop it, so that when Eduard put his hand on the directress's breast, he was merely submitting to an inevitable necessity.

The consequences of his action exceeded all expectations. As if by the wave of a magician's wand, the directress began to writhe in his arms, and in no time she had placed her hairy upper lip on his mouth. Then she dragged him onto the couch and wildly writhing and loudly sighing, bit his lip and the tip of his tongue, which hurt Eduard a lot. Then she slipped out of his arms, and said, "Wait!" and ran off to the bathroom.

Eduard licked his finger and found that his tongue was bleeding slightly. The bite hurt so much that his painstakingly induced intoxication receded, and once again his throat tightened from anxiety at the thought of what awaited him. From the bathroom could be heard a loud running and splashing of water. He picked up the bottle of cognac, put it to his lips, and drank deeply.

But by this time the directress had appeared in the doorway in a translucent nightgown (thickly decorated with lace over the breasts), and she was walking slowly toward Eduard. She embraced him. Then she stepped back and reproachfully asked: "Why are you still dressed?"

Eduard took off his jacket and, looking at the directress (who had her big eyes fixed on him), he couldn't think of anything but the fact that his body was likely to sabotage his assiduous will. Wishing therefore to arouse his body somehow or other, he said in an uncertain voice: "Undress completely."

With an abrupt and enthusiastically obedient movement she flung off her nightgown and bared her skinny white body, in the middle of which her thick black bush protruded in dreary abandon. She came slowly toward him, and with terror Eduard realized what he already knew: his body was completely fettered by anxiety.

I know, gentlemen, that in the course of the years you have become accustomed to the occasional insubordination of your own bodies, and that this no longer upsets you at all. But understand, Eduard was young then! His body's sabotage threw him into an incredible panic each time, and he bore it as an inexpiable disgrace, whether the witness to it was a beautiful face or one as hideous and comical as the directress's. The directress was now only a step away from him, and he, frightened and not knowing what to do, all at once said, he didn't even know how (it was the fruit of inspiration rather than of cunning reflection): "No, no! God, no! No, it is a sin, it would be a sin!" and he jumped away.

But the directress kept coming toward him, and she muttered: "What sin? There is no sin!"

Eduard retreated behind the table they had been sitting at a while before: "No, I can't do this. I don't have the right."

The directress pushed aside the armchair standing in her path, and went after Eduard, never taking her large dark eyes off him: "There is no sin! There is no sin!"

Eduard went around the table, behind him was only the couch and the directress was a mere step away. Now he could no longer escape, and it was probably his very desperation that made him at this moment of impasse to command her: "Kneel!"

She looked at him uncomprehendingly, but when he

repeated in a firm though desperate voice, "Kneel!" she enthusiastically fell to her knees in front of him and embraced his legs.

"Take those hands away," he called her to order. "Clasp them!"

Once again she looked at him uncomprehendingly.

"Clasp them! Did you hear?"

She clasped her hands.

"Pray!" he commanded.

She had her hands clasped, and she raised her eyes toward him fervently.

"Pray! So that God may forgive us," he shouted.

She had her hands clasped. She was looking up at him with her large eyes, and Eduard not only gained time, but looking down at her from above, he began to lose the oppressive feeling that he was merely her quarry, and he regained his self-assurance. He stepped back so that he could see all of her, and once again he commanded, "Pray!"

When she remained silent, he yelled: "Out loud!"

And the skinny, naked, kneeling woman began to recite: "Our Father, who art in heaven, hallowed be thy name, thy kingdom come . . ."

As she uttered the words of the prayer, she gazed up at him as if he were God himself. He watched her with growing pleasure: in front of him was kneeling the directress, being humiliated by a subordinate; in front of him a naked revolutionary was being humiliated by prayer; in front of him a praying woman was being humiliated by her nakedness.

This threefold image of humiliation intoxicated him, and something unexpected suddenly happened: his body revoked its passive resistance; Eduard had an erection!

As the directress said, "And lead us not into temptation," he quickly threw off all his clothes. When she said, "Amen," he violently lifted her off the floor and dragged her onto the couch.

9

That was on Thursday, and on Saturday Eduard went with Alice to the country to visit his brother, who welcomed them warmly and lent them the key to the nearby cottage.

The two lovers spent the whole afternoon wandering through the woods and meadows. They kissed, and Eduard's contented hands found that the imaginary line, level with her navel, which separated the sphere of innocence from that of fornication, didn't count anymore. At first he wanted to verify the long-awaited event verbally, but he became frightened of doing so and understood that he had best keep silent.

His judgment was probably correct; Alice's abrupt turnaround had occurred independently of his many weeks of persuasion, independently of his argumenta-

tion, independently of any *logical* consideration what-
soever. In fact it was based exclusively upon the news of
Eduard's martyrdom, consequently upon *a mistake*,
and it had been deduced quite *illogically* even from this
mistake; let us reflect for a moment: why should
Eduard's sufferings for his fidelity to his beliefs result
in Alice's infidelity to God's law? If Eduard had not
betrayed God before the fact-finding committee, why
should she now betray him before Eduard?

In such a situation any reflection expressed aloud
could risk revealing to Alice the inconsistency of her
attitude. So Eduard prudently kept silent, which went
unnoticed, because Alice herself kept chattering. She
was cheerful, and nothing indicated that this turnaround in her soul had been dramatic or painful.

When it got dark they went back to the cottage,
turned on the lights, turned down the bed, and kissed,
whereupon Alice asked Eduard to turn off the lights.
But the light of the stars continued to show through the
window, so Eduard had to close the shutters as well on
Alice's request. Then, in total darkness, Alice undressed
and gave herself to him.

Eduard had been looking forward to this moment for
so many weeks, but surprisingly enough, now, when it
was actually taking place, he didn't have the feeling
that it would be as significant as the length of time he
had been waiting for it suggested; it seemed to him so
easy and self-evident that during the act of love he was
almost distracted and was vainly trying to drive away
the thoughts that were running through his head:

everything came back to him, those long, futile weeks when Alice had tormented him with her coldness; the problems at school, which she had been the cause of, so instead of gratitude for her giving herself to him, he began to feel a kind of vindictive rancor. It irritated him how easily and without remorse she was now betraying her God Antifornicator, whom she had once so fanatically worshiped; it irritated him that no desire, no event, no upset troubled her serenity. It irritated him that she experienced everything without inner conflict, self-confidently and easily. And when this irritation threatened to overcome him with its power, he strove to make love to her passionately and furiously so as to force from her some sort of sound, moan, word, or pathetic cry, but he didn't succeed. The girl was quiet, and in spite of all his exertions in their lovemaking, it ended modestly and in silence.

Then she snuggled up against his chest and quickly fell asleep, while Eduard lay awake for a long time and realized that he felt no joy at all. He made an effort to imagine Alice (not her physical appearance but, if possible, her being in its entirety), and it occurred to him that he saw her *blurred*.

Let's stop at this word: Alice, as Eduard had seen her until this time, was, with all her naïveté, a stable and distinct being: the beautiful simplicity of her looks seemed to accord with the unaffected simplicity of her faith, and the simplicity of her destiny seemed to be the reason for her attitude. Until this time Eduard had seen her as solid and coherent: he could laugh at her, he could curse her, he could get around her with his guile, but (despite himself) he had to respect her.

Now, however, the unpremeditated snare of false news had caused a split in the coherence of her being, and it seemed to Eduard that her ideas were in fact only a *veneer* on her destiny, and her destiny only a veneer on her body; he saw her as an accidental conjunction of a body, ideas, and a life's course, an inorganic conjunction, arbitrary and unstable. He visualized Alice (who was breathing deeply on his shoulder), and he saw her body separately from her ideas, he liked this body, its ideas seemed ridiculous to him, and this body and its ideas formed no unity; he saw her as an ink line spreading on a blotter: without contours, without shape.

He really liked this body. When Alice got up in the morning, he forced her to remain naked, and, although just yesterday she had stubbornly insisted on closed shutters, for even the dim light of the stars had bothered her, she now altogether forgot her shame. Eduard was scrutinizing her (she cheerfully pranced around, looking for a package of tea and cookies for breakfast), and when Alice glanced at him after a moment, noticed that he was lost in thought. She asked him what was the matter. Eduard replied that after breakfast he had to go and see his brother.

His brother inquired how he was getting on at the school. Eduard replied that on the whole it was fine, and his brother said: "That Cechackova is a pig, but I forgave her long ago. I forgave her because she didn't know what she was doing. She wanted to harm me, but instead she helped me find a beautiful life. As a farmer I earn more, and contact with nature protects me from the skepticism to which citydwellers are prone."

"That woman, as a matter of fact, brought me some happiness too," said Eduard, lost in thought, and he told his brother that he had fallen in love with Alice, that he had feigned a belief in God, that he had had to appear before a committee, that Cechackova had wanted to reeducate him, and that Alice had finally given herself to him, thinking he was a martyr. The only thing he didn't tell was that he had forced the directress to recite the Lord's Prayer, because he saw disapproval in his brother's eyes. He stopped talking, and his brother said: "I may have a great many faults, but one I don't have: I've never dissimulated, and I've said to everyone's face what I thought."

Eduard loved his brother, and his disapproval hurt, so he made an effort to justify himself, and they began to argue. In the end Eduard said:

"I know you are a straightforward man and that you pride yourself on it. But put one question to yourself: *Why* in fact should one tell the truth? What obliges us to do it? And why do we consider telling the truth to be a virtue? Imagine that you meet a madman, who claims that he is a fish and that we are all fish. Are you going to argue with him? Are you going to undress in front of him and show him that you don't have fins? Are you going to say to his face what you think? Well, tell me!"

His brother was silent, and Eduard went on: "If you

told him the whole truth and nothing but the truth, only what you really thought, you would enter into a serious conversation with a madman and you yourself would become mad. And it is the same way with the world that surrounds us. If I obstinately told the truth to its face, it would mean that I was taking it seriously. And to take seriously something so unserious means to lose all one's own seriousness. I *have to* lie, if I don't want to take madmen seriously and become a madman myself."

10

It was Sunday afternoon, and the two lovers left for
town; they were alone in a compartment (the girl was
again chattering cheerfully), and Eduard remembered
how some time ago he had looked forward to finding in
Alice's *optional* character a seriousness that his duties
would never provide for him; and he sadly realized (as
the train idyllically clattered over the joints of the
tracks) that the love adventure he had experienced
with Alice was derisory, made up of chance and errors,
without any seriousness or meaning; he heard Alice's
words, he saw her gestures (she squeezed his hand),
and it occurred to him that these were signs devoid of
significance, currency without backing, weights made
of paper, and that he could not grant them value any
more than God could the prayer of the naked directress; and suddenly it seemed to him that, in fact, all
the people he had met in this town were only ink lines
spreading on a blotter, beings with interchangeable
attitudes, beings without firm substance; but what was
worse, what was far worse (it struck him next), was
that he himself was only a shadow of all these shadow-
characters; for he had been exhausting his own brain
only to adjust to them and imitate them and yet, even
if he imitated them with an internal laugh, not taking
them seriously, even if he made an effort to mock them
secretly (and so to justify his effort to adapt), it didn't
alter the case, for even malicious imitation remains

imitation, even a shadow that mocks remains a shadow, a secondary thing, derivative and wretched.

It was humiliating, terribly humiliating. The train idyllically clattered over the joints of the tracks (the girl was chattering) and Eduard said:

"Alice, are you happy?"

"Yes," said Alice.

"I'm miserable," said Eduard.

"What, are you crazy?" said Alice.

"We shouldn't have done it. It shouldn't have happened."

"What's gotten into you? You're the one who wanted to do it!"

"Yes, I wanted to," said Eduard. "But that was my greatest mistake, for which God will never forgive me. It was a sin, Alice."

"Come on, what's happened to you?" asked the girl calmly. "You yourself always said that God wants love most of all!"

When Eduard heard Alice, after the fact, quietly appropriating the theological sophistries with which he had so unsuccessfully taken the field a while ago, fury seized him: "I said that to test you. Now I've found out how faithful you are to God! And a person who is capable of betraying God is capable of betraying a man a hundred times more easily!"

Alice always found ready answers, but it would have been better for her if she hadn't, because they only provoked his vindictive rage. Eduard went on and on talking (in the end he used the words "nausea" and "physical disgust") until he did obtain from this placid and gentle face (finally!) sobs, tears, and moans.

"Goodbye," he said to her at the station, and he left her in tears. Only at home, several hours later, when this curious anger had subsided, did he understand all the consequences of what he had done: He imagined her body, which had pranced stark naked in front of him that morning, and when he realized that this beautiful body was lost to him because he himself, of his own free will, had driven it away, he called himself an idiot and had a mind to slap his own face.

But what had happened had happened, and it was no longer possible to change anything.

In order to be truthful, I must add that even if the idea of this beautiful body he had rejected caused Eduard a certain amount of grief, he coped with this loss fairly quickly. If the need for physical love had once tormented him and reduced him to a state of longing, it was the short-lived need of a recent arrival in the town. Eduard no longer suffered from this need. Once a week he visited the directress (habit had relieved his body of its initial anxieties), and he resolved to continue to visit her regularly until his position at the school was definitively clarified. Besides this, with increasing success he chased all sorts of other women and girls. As a consequence he began to appreciate far more the times when he was alone, and he became fond of solitary walks, which he sometimes combined (please devote a bit of attention to this detail) with a visit to the church.

No, don't worry, Eduard did not begin to believe in

God. I have no intention of crowning my story with such a flagrant paradox. But even if Eduard was almost certain that God did not exist, he turned toward the idea of God with yearning.

God is essence itself, whereas Eduard never found (and a number of years have passed since his adventures with the directress and with Alice) anything essential in his love affairs, or in his teaching, or in his thoughts. He is too honest to concede that he finds the essential in the unessential, but he is too weak not to long secretly for the essential.

Ah, ladies and gentlemen, a man lives a sad life when he cannot take anything or anyone seriously!

And that is why Eduard longs for God, for God alone is relieved of the distracting obligation of *appearing* and can merely *be*; for he alone constitutes (he alone, unique and nonexistent) the essential antithesis of this world, which is all the more existent for being unessential.

And so Eduard occasionally sits in church and looks dreamily at the cupola. Let us take leave of him at just such a time: It is afternoon, the church is quiet and empty. Eduard is sitting in a wooden pew and feeling sad at the thought that God does not exist. But just at this moment his sadness is so great that suddenly from its depth emerges the genuine *living* face of God. Look! It's true! Eduard is smiling! He is smiling, and his smile is happy.

Please keep him in your memory with this smile.

WRITTEN IN BOHEMIA BETWEEN 1958 AND 1968